"A man would be a fool, indeed, to ignore the warning signs."

He had recovered more quickly than she, but Kay rallied her defenses at that. What on earth did she think she was doing? And with *him* of all people? Self-disgust made her voice chilly. "There's no need, because we won't be seeing each other again after today."

"I sincerely hope not."

AMANDA BROWNING is a British author who was born and brought up in Essex, where she still lives. She has had a passion for books since she was a small child and worked as a librarian before she became a full-time writer. When she's not reading or writing she loves doing quizzes and embroidery. Her lively contemporary writing style appeals to readers everywhere.

Books by Amanda Browning

HARLEQUIN PRESENTS
1400—SOMETHING FROM THE HEART
1432—A PROMISE TO REPAY
1566—A TIME FOR LOVE
1677—AN OLD ENCHANTMENT
1724—SAVAGE DESTINY

Don't miss any of our special offers. Write to us at the following address for information on our newest releases.

Harlequin Reader Service
U.S.: 3010 Walden Ave., P.O. Box 1325, Buffalo, NY 14269
Canadian: P.O. Box 609, Fort Erie, Ont. L2A 5X3

AMANDA BROWNING

BROWNING

Trail of Love

Harlequin Books

TORONTO • NEW YORK • LONDON
AMSTERDAM • PARIS • SYDNEY • HAMBURG
STOCKHOLM • ATHENS • TOKYO • MILAN
MADRID • WARSAW • BUDAPEST • AUCKLAND

ISBN 0-373-11742-6

TRAIL OF LOVE

CHAPTER ONE

THE seat Kay Napier sat on so uncomfortably stood in the immaculately kept gardens of a quiet London square. Her large, troubled green eyes rested on the building opposite. Having come this far, it would be foolish not to go on, but the doubts which had been her disagreeable companions these last few weeks had risen up to hold her back. Did she really want to go in there and make a fool of herself? Yet wasn't it better to find out the truth? She sighed. What truth? The *truth* was that she was Kay Napier, a twenty-four-year-old actuary, and she shouldn't let one unpleasant incident make her doubt the beliefs of a lifetime.

Yet it had, and did, because sensible advice was very rarely taken. She needed to have her life put back into its proper perspective. She had believed there was nowhere she could go to achieve that, now her mother was dead, but a week ago the solution had hit her; there *was* somebody she could ask. The Endacotts themselves. The family lived in Northumbria, but Sir Charles Endacott was head of the family's merchant bank here in London. The very bank, in fact, that she sat across from now, trying to convince herself that she wasn't totally crazy.

When fate had produced a cancelled appointment, giving her some free hours in which to deal with her problem, her course of action had been clear. It still was, she thought with a wry smile, and recalled what Macbeth had said, 'If it were done when 'tis done, then 'twere well it were done quickly'. She would go in, get her answer, and then get on with the rest of her life.

With which bracing advice she climbed to her feet and headed for the gate set in the wrought-iron railings. The door to the elegant Regency building swished open almost soundlessly, which reminded Kay, although it was hardly necessary, that a great deal of money changed hands inside these portals.

The receptionist looked up with a friendly smile as Kay approached her desk. 'Can I help you?' she asked pleasantly.

Kay assumed her most businesslike expression. She might be in a quandary, but it wouldn't do to let anyone else know it. 'Yes. I would like to see Sir Charles Endacott, please.'

'Do you have an appointment?'

Mentally kicking herself for forgetting something so basic, Kay saw her spur-of-the moment project being scuttled before it reached first base. This now required some delicate handling, not to say outright bluff. Her smile was confident. 'No, I don't, but I'm sure you'll find he will see me.'

The young woman returned the smile with a polite one of her own. 'I'm sorry, but without an appointment Sir Charles doesn't see anyone,' she said firmly.

At any other time Kay would have admired her efficiency, but not today. 'I'm sure exceptions can be made?' Her glance said, surely, as one woman to another: we can come to some sort of arrangement.

'If you'd care to make an appointment, I'm sure Sir Charles will be only too happy to see you, *on that day*.'

Kay straightened her spine. She wasn't prepared to give in, now that she was here, and if it took a downright lie to get her past this female Cerberus, she'd use it. 'I'm sure he would, but he might not be too happy about missing me today!' she countered sweetly.

The receptionist was no fool, but at that implication she hesitated. 'I see.' She clearly wasn't too sure if she was hearing the truth but didn't want to take the risk of insulting a friend of her employer. 'You'll appreciate that Sir Charles is a very busy man. It may not be convenient. However, if you'll take a seat for a moment, I'll have a word with his secretary.'

Kay sank into a seat by the window, marvelling at her own temerity. She watched as the receptionist held a low-voiced conversation on the telephone. Was she being described? she wondered, and shivered. It could be from nerves, or the building's air-conditioning, which was working flat out because this was one of the hottest summers on record. The heat troubled her, for her skin was so fair that it simply burned instead of tanning. It was a legacy of her rich copper-coloured hair, which, when free of its confining French pleat, fell in lush waves to her shoulders.

She had wanted to look smart, yet cool, and she knew the grey linen pencil skirt with matching jacket suited her tall, slim figure. There had been times when she had described her figure as boyish, but that was no longer true. Her hips might be narrow, but her legs were long and shapely. Her breasts were undoubtedly small, but they were in perfect proportion to the rest of her. There could be no doubting her femininity.

A slight frown marred the perfection of her finely boned face as she dropped her gaze to the manila folder she held on her lap. Even white teeth chewed uneasily at lips that usually described a perfect, if slightly full bow. The source of all her recent uncertainty lay inside.

As if to reassure herself that she hadn't dreamed it all, she reached inside and withdrew a folded paper. It was her birth certificate, and although she virtually knew the details by heart she still opened it. Sarah Jane Napier, born twenty-four years ago to Ronald and Jean Napier.

Nobody called her Sarah, of course, but she had always known the reason for that—or thought she had. Kay had been a pet name, a fancy of her mother's which had stuck. There was nothing unusual in that. But then she hadn't been in possession of her mother's diary. Or that letter, which she had destroyed but somehow couldn't forget.

Just then she heard the receptionist put the receiver down, and, quickly tucking the paper away, Kay rose and approached the desk once more. The young woman was extremely polite.

'Sorry to keep you waiting. If you take the lift to the top floor, Mrs Rivers will meet you.'

Kay saved her smile until she was inside the lift. So far so good. However, it was only a small success. She was to be met, which meant they weren't giving her the chance to go anywhere they didn't want her to. She'd have to think fast. This Mrs Rivers sounded a very different kettle of fish. All the same she found herself quite looking forward to the encounter.

She laughed. Lance would have a fit at her behaviour! That brought her up short. Lance Young was the man she expected to marry one day, yet she hadn't even discussed this visit with him. She hadn't wanted to bother him. Now it occurred to her to question why not.

She realised she'd said nothing because he'd only call her foolish. Lance was a very meticulous, private man in his late thirties. He respected her sensible outlook, her career-mindedness. This—sudden insecurity—he would think frivolous. Instinctively she had kept her own counsel. And, if the fact that she couldn't confide in him her personal worries hurt, the disappointment was small, for in everything else they were like-minded. Neither believed in a 'grand passion'. Their marriage would be one of mutual respect. It had always given Kay a sense of well-being to know where her life was going.

Seconds after that warming thought raised her spirits, the lift doors opened again to reveal Sir Charles's doughty secretary. Mrs Rivers was a compact, grey-haired woman who was friendly enough in an impersonal way. She led Kay to her office before opening the attack.

'I understand that you wish to see Sir Charles, but there seems to be some confusion as to whether you have an appointment or not.' The secretary consulted an open diary on her desk briefly.

Kay assumed a cajoling smile. 'I don't have one, but...'

'But apparently that isn't necessary because Sir Charles is an old acquaintance,' the sentence was finished for her.

With her bluff called, Kay was left in a difficult position. To say yes and get caught out in the lie would, she suspected, earn her short shrift, whereas the truth... Yet what choice did she have? 'Actually, he isn't,' she admitted wryly. 'I know it was wrong to lie, but I only did it because it really is so vitally important that I see him.'

Mrs Rivers resumed her seat. 'That's as may be. As a statement it's hardly unique. The fact remains that Sir Charles is a very busy man.'

'I appreciate that, I really do, but I only need to see him for five minutes, ten at the most,' she insisted pleadingly.

The older woman sighed and pursed her lips. 'Well...perhaps if you were to tell me what your business is?' she offered reluctantly.

Kay had no wish to reveal anything unless she had to. 'It's a personal matter.'

Sir Charles's secretary regarded her askance. 'Can't you be more specific?'

Shaking her head, Kay squared up. 'The only person I *can* explain it to is Sir Charles. Can he fit me in, do you think?'

Mrs Rivers looked at her squarely for almost a minute, then sighed again. 'You're very persistent. I'll see what I can do. All I can promise you is a long wait with no guarantee.'

That was all Kay wanted—a chance. 'I'll wait.'

The secretary smiled wryly. 'You may live to regret saying that. Why don't you make yourself comfortable over there?' She indicated a low couch nestling behind a coffee-table on which lay several magazines. 'I'll let you know if Sir Charles will see you.'

Kay flashed her a smile and once more took a seat. She picked up a magazine and began to flip through it, but, having come so close to her goal, it was impossible to think of anything but the reason she was there. That, of course, was the diary.

Kay sighed at the memories that brought. There had only been the two of them since her father left them when she was only a baby, and her mother's tragically early death from cancer had been a blow, so suddenly had it happened. It had left Kay with the sad task of clearing her mother's house, and she had come across the diary at the bottom of a case containing various other personal items. These she had taken home with her to go through at another time. Only the diary had called for her attention. She had read it in the expectation of finding out more about her mother's early life—a subject she had been reticent about—but the entries had been spasmodic, covering no more than a few years at most, the pages crossed in a small neat hand.

They had begun with her daughter's birth. The entry was simple: 'K came today. She's so beautiful'. The wording had not struck her then, nor the singularity of her name only being referred to by the initial. But even that wasn't so very unusual for someone keeping a diary, and Kay had forgotten about it until, several weeks later, her interest had been piqued by a television documentary on kidnapped children who had never been returned after the ransom had been paid. One case which had featured prominently was that of Kimberley Endacott.

A passing interest it might have remained, but for the anonymous letter. Addressed to her mother and re-directed from her house to Kay's flat, it had demanded money, said the writer would be in touch, and had contained clippings of the very same Kimberley Endacott case.

She had assumed it was the work of a crank, and torn it up angrily, refusing to give it credence, until one evening she had answered the telephone. The caller had asked for Jean, and when she had told him her mother had died, he had demanded to know if Jean had read the clippings.

'No,' Kay had told him with satisfaction. 'I tore them up. Mother died several weeks ago, so you're too late with your sleazy attempt to blackmail her!' she had declared coldly and slammed the receiver down.

Only the call had added substance to the letter and somehow she couldn't stop thinking about it. In the end she had had to go to the library and get photocopies of the clippings and then read the diary again.

Things had started to click in her mind. At first she had laughed it off as preposterous. It was only a co-incidence that the first entry was on the same day as little Kimberley had disappeared. That the ransom had been paid and collected on the day her father had left them. That Kay was an odd name to call a child christened Sarah, and that the initial 'K' could refer to Kimberley as much as it did Kay.

All coincidences, and yet they had preyed on her mind. Because if, by the wildest stretch of the imagination, it should be true, then that could make her gentle, hard-working mother a kidnapper. For that was what the anonymous letter had surely been implying.

A thought that made her feel as if a gaping hole had opened up beneath her feet. A thought so alarming that she had dismissed it as ludicrous. This had happened in the north of England, and she had lived in London all her life. No! She was Kay Napier, an actuary, aged twenty-four. Her birth certificate said so. It also, dismayingly, gave an address in Alnwick.

Then the doubts had resurged. 'What if?' nagged at her day and night. Questions crowded in, but there were no answers, and no one to ask. Disloyalty and guilt at what she was allowing herself to suspect of someone who had shown her nothing but love warred with an increasing need to know. Which was why she had screwed her courage to the sticking place and come here today. Because a university degree and a down-to-earth job as an actuary in a highly reputable firm in the city couldn't allay her primal fear. She knew it wouldn't go from her mind until she had a definite 'no'.

At which point she dragged her thoughts back to the present. Time passed slowly, and she had drunk a cup of coffee and flipped through two magazines before the secretary, who had slipped discreetly through a door, reappeared and beckoned her over.

'Sir Charles has agreed to give you five minutes. Go on through.' She nodded to the open door. With a fast-beating heart, Kay stepped into the inner sanctum.

Sir Charles Endacott was sitting at a large desk by the window. Now in his seventies, he still possessed a full head of hair, although it was silvery grey, like his moustache. Puffing on a pipe, he watched Kay approach him through sharp grey eyes.

Kay stared at him as he rose to his feet and waved a hand in the direction of a chair. It struck her then, that the question she was about to ask had far-reaching implications. This man, this stranger, could be her grandfather! And that really was absurd, because she felt nothing. There was nothing in his distinguished face that reminded her of herself.

It was enough to clear her vision and to tell her that coming here was totally preposterous. She wasn't an Endacott, she knew it in her bones. Realising her foolishness in allowing one malicious person to manipulate her, she hesitated with her hand on the back of the chair. It would take some doing now, to extricate herself from this with her dignity intact.

'Well, young woman?' Sir Charles prompted in a brisk voice. 'My secretary tells me you insisted on seeing me. Did you think I would be flattered that such a lovely young thing should seek my advice on something personal? Unfortunately I can't say I approve of your methods. Do you make a habit of thrusting your way into people's offices?'

Kay wished the floor could open up, and horrified colour washed into her cheeks because, after all her wangling, she knew she was wasting his time. 'I'm most terribly sorry, but I'm afraid I've made a mistake.'

Grey eyes narrowed. 'Have you indeed? Am I to take it you didn't wish to see me?'

'No! That is, I thought...' she began disjointedly, only to be halted by his abruptly raised hand.

Sir Charles began by frowning, then a look of dawning comprehension swept across his features. 'Ah,' he said, and reached for the telephone, punching out a number. 'Ben? Get in here, would you?' he ordered down the line before replacing the receiver and eyeing her unwaveringly.

Perplexed by this seemingly illogical action, and not sure if it was a dismissal or not, Kay began a diplomatic retreat. 'You're busy. I'm sorry. I'll just...' The sound of the door opening behind her halted the flow, and she turned.

'What's this all about, Charles?' a smooth male voice queried, punctuating the question with the closing of the door.

The man advancing into the room was in his midthirties, tall, six feet at least, and slim of hip. Even the most conservative of suits couldn't hide the lean muscularity of his frame, nor the almost cat-like quality of his movements. Kay suffered an unfamiliar tightening

of her stomach muscles. Out of the blue, her senses were
bombarded with messages that set her nerves tingling
and her heart thumping. She raised her eyes to his
handsome face. He had the bluest eyes she had ever seen,
and his mouth was a criminal temptation. Set in a strong
face, surrounded by thick waves of black hair, they were
an attraction she recognised with a shock. Potent and
heady as the finest wine.

But there was more to come. Because for a moment
their eyes met, and clashed, and something like a bolt
of lightning shot through her. The shock she knew to
be on her face was duplicated on his. She could see the
fine tension in him suddenly. It had been total recognition. Elemental and instant.

Yet while she was trying to assimilate it, his eyes lifted
to her bright copper hair, where they lingered. The
change in him was instantaneous. For a second he sent
her a fulminating glare which was doused by the appearance of a cynical smile on his lips. Automatically
she braced herself, without knowing why.

'Now then, young woman,' Sir Charles reclaimed her
attention. 'This is Ben Radford. I expect he's the man
you expected to see, isn't he?' Clearly he found it
amusing, although the man who stopped beside him,
arms crossed, wasn't laughing.

His, 'I hardly think so, Charles,' mingled with her,
'I beg your pardon?'

From the name she recognised the younger man as the
other partner in the bank. He was well-known and respected in the City, and was widely suspected to be the
real motivator behind the bank's continued success.
Which was well enough, but she was at a loss to understand why Sir Charles should imagine *she* wanted to see
him.

There followed a brief pause when they all looked at
each other. Sir Charles frowned and Ben Radford's eyes
were cold. Kay found herself stiffening defensively.

The older man cleared his throat. 'You mean she isn't one of your damn flirtations?'

Kay was far from amused to find herself lumped in with a host of women who apparently chased after Ben Radford, even though, after her own response, she could understand why they did it. No wonder he was looking down his elegant nose at her. 'There seems to be some mistake,' she said frostily, dispelling the idea immediately.

'And you made it,' Ben Radford cut in swiftly, making her gasp. Who did he think he was? Handsome is as handsome does, she thought, and he falls a long way short. Of all the conceit!

Sir Charles was none too pleased either, but for apparently different reasons. 'Ben!' he remonstrated, but the younger man remained unperturbed.

'What does she want?' he asked shortly, and in a tone guaranteed to put her back up. Even if she weren't a redhead, with all the temper that implied.

Kay focused narrowed eyes on him, angry for herself and Sir Charles, who was a true gentleman. 'Nothing. I've already said I made a mistake. I was about to leave.'

That cynical smile deepened. 'Yet you obviously came here with some purpose in mind.'

On her mettle, Kay raised her chin, refusing to be browbeaten by his look or tone of voice. 'Yes, I did. There *was* a question I intended to ask Sir Charles, but I changed my mind.' Let him make what he liked of that, she thought. Clearly his character wasn't as attractive as his looks.

'Really?' he scoffed.

Her anger, hinted at by her hair, but usually kept under wraps, boiled up. 'Yes, really!' she snapped back.

Sir Charles banged his pipe down. 'Stop harassing the girl, Ben!' he ordered, and the younger man took his eyes from her briefly. Kay experienced a shaky kind of relief, only now aware of the quality of tension that had crackled between them. It was to be short-lived.

'Charles, the girl is a redhead. A strawberry blonde, if I'm not mistaken,' he said incisively.

There was a tangible change in atmosphere. Something new and disquieting had entered the lists against her. Automatically Kay raised a hand to her glittering locks as two pairs of eyes speared her. 'I fail to see what that has to do with it,' she argued, very aware of a pronounced chill in the air.

'Do you, Miss...? Do you have a name, I wonder, or should I guess?' Ben Radford probed scathingly.

Kay wondered how she could, even for a second, have found that cynical face attractive. 'My name is Kay Napier,' she replied with seething dignity.

'What was the question you wanted to ask me, Miss Napier?' There was a reserve in Sir Charles's voice now, and she found that strangely upsetting. His innate courtesy remained, but Ben Radford's insidious cynicism had poisoned his mind against her—and for no good reason that she could see. Her emergent dislike of him intensified.

She shook her head, unable to blame Sir Charles. 'It's not important,' she temporised, and she should have known she wouldn't be allowed to get away with it.

'It was important enough to bring you here. Why don't you ask it and let us be the judges?' Ben Radford commanded in a tone that brooked no argument.

She produced a smile that was every bit as cynical as his. As a judge he had already shown that his impartiality was seriously compromised. The tension now filling the room was awesome, and Kay had no idea what it was she had done to produce such a reaction. Surely not just the fact of having red hair? There was more here than met the eye, and she wouldn't have been human if she hadn't wanted to know what it was. The way to find out was to ask the question she had come here for.

'Very well, though it's a waste of your time because I already know I was a fool,' she declared pointedly. 'You'll think so too.'

'Oh, I doubt very much if that will be our reaction, Miss Napier,' her antagonist drawled with heavy irony.

She bluntly ignored him, turning instead to the older man, who had sunk down into his seat. However, voicing the question was no easier now than it would have been five minutes ago. 'Sir Charles, my name is Kay Napier— well, it's Sarah really, but everyone calls me Kay. I'm twenty-four years old. I have my birth certificate here telling me all this. But...' She really didn't want to mention the letter in the other man's hearing, especially as she had destroyed it. 'My mother died not long ago, and in among her things I found her diary. This is the crazy part. In the diary she used "K", you see, just the initial. I thought it stood for Kay, but what if...?' Helplessly she floundered to a halt, then, with eyes as much angry as unconsciously confused, added, 'Oh, this is ridiculous. Just tell me this—could I be Kimberley Endacott?'

CHAPTER TWO

WHATEVER reaction she had expected to receive, the total silence that followed wasn't it. She would have anticipated anger, or even dismay, at her intrusion on a subject so personally tragic. It was Ben Radford whose deep blue eyes registered withering contempt.

'Who sent you, Miss Napier?' he demanded in a voice that could cut through three-quarter-inch steel.

Already made uncomfortable by her own sense of betrayal and confusion, she found his insinuation doubly distasteful. Consequently her voice dripped ice. 'Nobody sent me. I came here because...' Her hesitation was fractional as she veered once more from the full truth. 'Ever since I saw that programme I've been unable to think of anything else.' She answered him, but her eyes were on the still silent older man, who now appeared lost in thought.

Ben Radford laughed harshly. 'You and thousands like you! Have you any idea how many claimants have beaten a path to our door since Kimberley disappeared?'

She shot him a glare. 'I don't care about them!' she gritted, so angry at him that she entirely missed the point of his question.

His smile grew wolfish. 'You should. They all had the same idea as you—getting their hands on the Endacott fortune.'

Now *that* did get through. Kay blinked like a startled owl, the colour draining from her cheeks. 'What?' She was shocked, her thoughts so far removed from the fiscal. He couldn't possibly be thinking...

18

Ben Radford rounded the desk in two purposeful strides, to loom over her like some threatening bird of prey, and against her will she backed away. But only one step before stiffening her spine and squaring up to him. Not at all an easy thing to do, because his potency at the width of a room seemed to treble at such close quarters. He was not the sort of man you could ever ignore, even if he weren't as handsome as sin. Battling regrettably capricious senses, she forced herself to concentrate on his words, and not the attractive curve of his mouth.

'Had she been here, Kimberley Endacott would have been twenty-four and shortly to come into possession of a substantial amount of money. Which, naturally, you didn't know,' he finished scornfully.

She held her ground, her body trembling. She told herself it was anger—only anger. Because she had never been so insulted in her life before. 'No, I didn't, and it's not why I'm here!' she protested her innocence gamely. He didn't believe her, and, in fairness, if what he said was true, why should he? Desperate to remove her gaze from one that had almost an hypnotic effect, she turned to the desk. 'Sir Charles, just tell me there's no possible way I could be Kimberley, and I'll leave.'

A snort echoed behind her. 'That's certainly a novel angle. I don't believe anyone else has used it,' Ben Radford drawled nastily, and Kay, pushed to the limit, lost her temper.

She swung round, eyes flashing fire, hands balled into fists at her sides. 'Shut up!' she ordered, then balked at her nerve.

His brows rose. 'Well, well. To use an overworked cliché, you're magnificent when you're angry.'

It could have been a compliment, but it wasn't. She had never come so close to actually hitting a man, but the temptation was great. It successfully negated her sense of contrition at her behaviour towards him. 'I came here because I was concerned, not to hear your ridiculous accusations.' Once more she turned her back and appealed to Sir Charles. 'Please, look at me. I can't be your granddaughter, can I? The whole idea is ludicrous, isn't it? Just tell me so, so that I can stop thinking these terrible thoughts about someone I loved very dearly.'

Sir Charles glanced up at that and heaved a deep sigh. 'I'm afraid I cannot do so. I've no more idea than anyone as to whether my granddaughter is alive. As to what she would look like now—you could be her. The colouring is right.'

This wasn't what she wanted to hear at all. 'You can't be serious!' she gasped in dismay.

There was a flicker of compassion in the old grey eyes as he pushed himself rather tiredly to his feet. 'I can sympathise with your problem, Miss Napier. You're being made to doubt where only trust had been. You want that trust restored. However, you'll appreciate, too, my own dilemma. I could walk past Kimberley in the street tomorrow and not know her.'

The unspoken anguish in that soft statement moved her terribly. Beside it, her own doubts seemed selfishly trivial. 'I'm sorry. I never meant to revive bad memories for you. It was simply that I didn't know who else to ask,' she apologised stiffly, voice tinged with regret.

Sir Charles circled his desk and laid a large, comforting hand on her shoulder. 'You haven't upset me, if that troubles you. One doesn't ever forget. One simply goes on living.'

To one side, his partner snorted. 'Charles, you're letting a pretty face undermine your judgement. Any minute now you'll be offering to take her to lunch!'

'Don't be so damned cynical, Ben. The girl's upset. Any fool can see that,' Sir Charles countered irascibly.

Bed Radford dragged an irate hand through his hair. 'And there's no fool like an old fool!' he rejoined, then held up a placatory hand as he saw the older man bristle.

'OK, I'm sorry. You'll do as you please, but just don't forget she probably knows all the angles, and *I* know what she's angling for.' His blue eyes flashed a warning at her that made her shiver. It said: You may fool Charles, but you don't fool me for one minute. 'As I seem to be an unwanted third in this little drama, I might as well be on my way.' However, at the door he halted. 'But I will offer you a small piece of advice, Miss Napier. You'd do well to look up the law on blackmail. I'm sure you'll find it fascinating reading.' His pithy parting shot made her go cold.

'You mustn't mind Ben, he's only looking after my interests. I'm afraid you aren't the first young woman to turn up, but you are the only one who wanted us to prove you *weren't* Kimberley.'

Regaining her composure now that the other man had gone, taking the tension with him, she looked serious. 'Please believe me, I never once thought about the money.'

He smiled. 'No doubt Ben would call me a fool again, but I do believe you.'

Kay smiled back. He really was a very nice man, unlike his younger partner. 'Thank you,' she said, and would have taken her leave, only a thought occurred to her. 'If I had come here, claiming to be Kimberley, what would you have done?'

'Called the police,' he proclaimed, not mincing his words.

'Oh!' she responded, disconcerted, realising he might be kind but he wasn't a fool. She had got off very lightly. Far more lightly than his partner would have liked.

'You mustn't forget my granddaughter was kidnapped and my family blackmailed for a very large sum of money. Both of which, and to our continuing sadness in one case, we have never seen again.'

Kay knew an enormous sense of guilt at bringing the whole tragic episode to the fore again. 'I'm sorry, I never meant to cause you any distress. It was selfish of me, and stupid, too. I know who I am, and I shouldn't have allowed a string of coincidences to undermine that. Please forgive me.'

Sir Charles escorted her to the door. 'Of course I will, my dear. What are you going to do now?'

She hoped he wasn't about to offer her lunch as Ben Radford had so cynically suggested. She gave a tiny shrug. 'Go back to Winterbourne and Stonely, and put this entire episode behind me.'

Sir Charles looked impressed. 'They're very sound. A good financial reputation. What do you do there?'

There had been times in her life when explaining her work had been a complete turn-off, but she didn't fear that from this man. 'I'm an actuary. Basically I'm an investment analyst, managing portfolios and such.'

He whistled soundlessly. 'If I say I'm impressed, it is sincerely meant. That's quite a position for one so young.'

Kay grimaced. Her comparative youth, combined with her sex, did have its drawbacks. After failing to get jobs she was eminently qualified for, it had dawned on her that her looks were decidedly against her. Which was why she now dressed in very businesslike suits and drew her hair back. Experience had taught her it inspired confidence in her clients, and her employers.

Sir Charles opened the door, and Kay stepped outside, finding herself back in the corridor. She smiled up at him ruefully. 'I'm working on getting older,' she quipped, then sobered with a sigh. 'You must think I'm a very ungrateful daughter who could think such things of my mother.'

'A minute or two in a lifetime is no crime. We're all human, and make mistakes. Good luck to you, Miss Napier.'

'And to you,' she said, and on a rare impulse, reached up to brush a swift kiss on his weathered cheek. Then, a little embarrassed, she turned and walked back towards the lift. She had made rather a fool of herself, but she would recover from it. At least there had been one positive result—common sense had returned at last, despite the lack of confirmation, and it was as if a weight had been lifted from her shoulders, giving a spring to her step.

'Very touching!'

The sarcastically drawled comment brought her head round and she found herself confronting a stony-faced Bed Radford.

'Laying claim, were you?' he went on, joining her as she waited for the lift to arrive.

Kay went instantly tense and on the defensive. Oh, he was handsome, but there wasn't an ounce of compassion or understanding in him. 'Actually, I was *dis*claiming.'

As the lift doors opened, he stepped aside with studied gallantry, and she ground her teeth, stepping into the small cubicle. It shrank alarmingly as he followed her, stabbing at the button with a viciousness that was the only sign of the anger he was concealing.

'Very clever. Now Charles won't be able to think of anything else. He'll begin to wonder. Then he'll contact you. No doubt you told him where you could be reached?' He saw her involuntary start and his lip curled.

Kay rushed to her own defence. 'That wasn't why I told him.'

'But it was why you kissed him!' he charged caustically.

Their eyes met across the small space, and there it was again—a charge so powerful that it was as if she had been plugged into the mains. It left her tingling, all the fine hairs on her skin raised to attention. That he had felt it too was in the wide flaring of his nostrils as he breathed in swiftly. It became of vital importance to hide a reaction that astounded her.

'I was saying goodbye!' she snapped in a rising voice, and her nerves jolted violently as his hand flashed out to press the stop button and the lift ceased its smooth descent. Alarm jangled through her, and there was no way to stop her heart from thudding against her ribs.

'Is that how you usually say goodbye to virtual strangers?' Ben Radford derided.

It had been an impulsive act that she couldn't regret enough, now she knew it had been witnessed. 'To an elderly gentleman who showed me olde-worlde courtesy, yes!' she countered, tremblingly aware of his impressive bulk, and the anger and dislike emanating from him in waves.

But it still couldn't conquer dismayingly receptive senses. Having scarcely registered before, they now appeared ultra-sensitive. His aftershave was tangy and inviting. In a seeming reversal of roles, everything about him was a siren-song, calling to her on a level as primitive as the emotions it aroused.

'And I suppose you had no ulterior motive in mind?' His question was a welcome distraction to her thoughts.

Somehow she managed to instil scorn into her tone. 'Don't judge me by your own yardstick. Now, if you've had your fun, Mr Radford, let me out,' she added curtly as she braced herself to meet his eyes.

'Why do you do it?' he returned, making no move to comply, and effectively blocking her escape by resting back against the control panel.

Kay blinked, put off stride. 'Do what?'

'Dress like my maiden aunt, Miss Prunes and Prisms.'

She balked at that. 'Don't be so damned insulting! I dress this way because it pleases me!' Not for anything would she explain herself to him.

He eyed her up and down. 'Well, it sure as hell doesn't please me,' he observed disparagingly.

'You can't know how delighted I am to hear that, Mr Radford,' she responded with sarcastic relish, only to have the feeling shattered seconds later.

'Does it please any man, I wonder?'

The man was insufferable! 'For your information, it does!' she retorted, then could have kicked herself for descending to his level.

'What's he got, starch in his veins, too?' he mocked.

Kay bit back a scathing retort, satisfying herself with a pithy, 'Whatever Lance has got, it's a one-hundred-per-cent improvement on you!'

A smile curved his lips. 'Sounds as if you're trying to convince yourself more than me. Does he know you're here?'

She couldn't help the betraying flicker of her lashes. 'This is a private matter,' she snapped defensively.

'Wouldn't he approve of your methods?' he chided.

Lance wouldn't, but for different reasons entirely from, those this man imagined. Not that she'd ever tell him that. 'You made up your mind about me before I ever said a word, and that's that, isn't it?' she charged instead.

'What else did you expect me to do?'

'At least give me a fair hearing.'

'Oh, I listened, lady, and I didn't like what I heard. What made you think you could get away with it? Because Charles is an old man, or because you have that extraordinary shade of hair?'

That was the second time he'd referred to her hair, and it annoyed her as much as it mystified her. 'Why do you keep saying that? Why is my hair so damned important?' she challenged touchily, having suffered as most redheads did from teasing.

His eyes grew mockingly sceptical. 'Do you really expect me to believe you don't know?'

This time she held on to her temper. 'Why would I ask if I knew?'

'Because you're clever. To know too little is far more plausible than to know too much,' he explained in that hateful drawl.

Kay followed his reasoning all too clearly. 'If I was trying to prove I was Kimberley Endacott, which I'm not.'

'Ah, but we only have your word for that,' he countered. 'The same way I only have your word that you didn't know Marsha Endacott was a redhead, and her mother, too. They were renowned for it. There's a famous portrait of the two of them at the house, but I doubt you'll ever get to see it,' he added with a certain satisfaction.

Kay stared at him for a moment, to check if he was lying, but in truth, she already knew he wasn't. She closed her eyes. Why had he had to tell her that? She had come here, certain of having her doubts allayed, and they had been—until this very moment. Why couldn't he have let sleeping dogs lie?

When she looked at him again, it was through stormy sea-green eyes. 'I want to leave,' she reiterated quietly, 'and I'd rather not cause a scene if I can avoid it.'

His head went back at the threat, yet he turned and pushed the button none the less. However, when the doors opened on the ground floor mere seconds later, he halted her departure with a firm hand on her arm. It was like being branded. To all intents and purposes, the sleeve of her jacket need not have existed. She felt the impact to her core and caught her breath at the shock of it. His words seemed to come from a long way away.

'Stay away from the Endacotts. They've suffered enough. I'm giving you fair warning, Miss Napier. Continue in this, and I'll take it as personal, and believe me you'll regret that. Have I made myself clear?'

Kay controlled her skittering senses with an effort and shivered, knowing he was not a man to make idle threats.

'Perfectly,' she gritted, and looked pointedly at his restraining hand.

He seemed to release her arm reluctantly. 'Good, because I'd really hate for someone as lovely as you to get hurt.'

Disbelievingly, she made the mistake of meeting his gaze. His eyes were no longer cool. They blazed, but not with anger, and they both froze. Slowly, almost incredulously, he raised a hand to stroke a finger down the fragile line of her cheek.

Kay felt that brief caress to her bones. It was like a lick of flame. Her shiver this time had nothing to do with fear, and her lids dropped. Something was happening between them that was way beyond her experience, and instinctively she fought it. 'I'm touched by your concern,' she retorted with all the sarcasm she could muster. 'Now let me go!' The order held a quiet desperation as she felt the situation slipping out of her control.

He did no such thing, and it seemed to Kay almost as if he couldn't. 'I can feel you trembling,' he declared in an oddly strained voice.

Kay drew in a ragged breath, as the suggestion triggered off a shock wave through her system. 'If I am, it's because I detest you,' she choked out, looking away, sensing freedom a step away yet unable to reach it. Then her eyes were drawn helplessly back to him. Something he saw there made his fingers tighten.

'Not that. You're afraid. What do you think I'm going to do to you?' he asked dulcetly, as if he'd entirely forgotten where they were.

'I'm not afraid,' she denied thickly. 'I just want to say goodbye, Mr Radford.'

He drew in an audible breath. 'They say you're only afraid of what you don't know,' he murmured, almost to himself. As if he had to convince himself of something.

In the next instant every nerve in her body quivered with shock. He caught her to him, one hand curving about her jaw as the other encircled her waist and gathered her fast to his strong male body. Her gasp died under his descending mouth.

After a moment's frozen surprise, she began to struggle for freedom. But trying to drag her mouth free only made him slide his free hand into her hair to hold her still. It was the most incredible thing, for as his fingers slid through her hair, running over her scalp, *frissons* of excitement brought the hairs up all over her body, and she shivered. Time and space became encapsulated. She forgot to fight because too many other messages were shooting to her brain. How his solidity had a potency she could never have dreamed of. That her breasts found the feel of that strength incredibly exciting, and flowered into aching points that wanted to press closer.

And his mouth... No kiss had ever made her feel so hot and shivery at the same time. As if she had a fever. His lips scorched her with their dry heat. Moving sensually, he tasted her, one second barely brushing her lips, the next drawing her lower lip into his mouth, caressing the silky inner skin with his tongue. Ever gradually the kiss deepened, demanding more of a response—and getting it. Until finally her lips parted, and with a triumphant sound he claimed her with his tongue piratically plundering her sweetness until her own tongue flickered to meet his.

Then, as suddenly as it had begun, it was over. Raising his head, he eased away to look down into her flushed face.

'What are you, some sort of witch?' he demanded in a husky drawl.

She shuddered in reaction. If she was, then he was a wizard. She'd never felt such magic. 'I...think you'd better let me go,' she responded weakly, somehow unable to free herself.

For a moment it seemed he hadn't heard her, then with a sort of mental shake he released her and stepped back. 'You're right, of course. You're trouble with a capital T. A man would be a fool indeed to ignore the warning signs.'

He had recovered quicker than she, but Kay rallied her defences at that. What on earth did she think she was doing? And with him of all people? Self-disgust made her voice chilly. 'There's no need, because we won't be seeing each other again after today.'

'I sincerely hope not.'

Kay winced inwardly as he made it abundantly clear he deplored that moment of weakness. Well, she did, too, and she let him know it. 'No more than I. *Goodbye*, Mr Radford. I won't say it's been a pleasure meeting you, because I hate lying.'

Without another word she turned and marched away, very much aware that his eyes were on her until she passed through the front door. Only out on the pavement again did she draw in a fresh breath, and found she was shaking. As much from sheer reaction as anger. Not caring where she went, she strode out, her pace mirroring her inner turmoil. Her response to Ben Radford filled her mind. She had always thought she had a low sex drive, but he had proved that notion as full of holes as a rusty pail.

Reviewing her life now, she realised she must have led a very cloistered existence to have arrived at that decision about herself. Or had she begun to believe her own publicity? Had her well-cut businesslike suits and dresses become so much a part of her that the sensual side of herself had been hidden from her? Until her encounter with Ben Radford had proved there was nothing staid in her make-up—when the right man triggered her natural responses.

Yet, while he had done that, he was the *wrong* man. He hadn't wanted to feel that way about her any more than she had him, so why had it stung, the way he had chosen to fight it? Did the answer really matter anyway? His opinion of her and her 'questionable motives' should be enough to make her head easily conquer her wayward emotions.

Besides, there was Lance. He was solid and dependable. OK, so he had never lit any fires in her, but she hadn't expected him to. How 'real' was it, anyway? Emotions were fickle. It had been a very emotional day. Her reaction was probably heightened by the unreality of the whole situation. The thought somewhat eased her troubled spirit.

Her footsteps slowed, and, glancing round, she discovered she had no idea where she was. Fortunately a taxi cruised into sight and she flagged it down. Giving the driver the office address, she sank back into the seat with a sigh. She thanked heaven she would never have to see Ben Radford again. She would put him from her mind, just as she intended doing with the sad business of Kimberley Endacott.

Two days later, as Kay was congratulating herself on her success—the diary once more resided in the case which now lay tucked away at the back of her wardrobe—she glanced up quickly as, after only a brief knock, her office door was pushed open.

'Do you have a minute, Kay?' John Kovacs, her immediate boss, asked as he popped his bald head through the gap.

'For you, five,' she returned with a grin. 'What can I do for you?' she enquired as he came in and sat down. His usual jovial face was glum.

'A big favour, I hope. You know I wouldn't ask this if it weren't so important. There's a VIP due to meet Matthew Winterbourne about now, only he's in a jam somewhere between here and Heathrow. There's been a monumental foul-up somewhere, and, what's worse, we can't contact the VIP to put him off.'

Kay could see what was coming. 'And you want me to keep him entertained until Matthew gets here?'

John's face began to beam. 'I knew we could count on you!' he declared, jumping up.

'Hey, I haven't said I'll do it yet,' Kay pointed out quickly, then almost laughed, because if John had had any hair left he would have been pulling it out. So, although the request smacked of male chauvinism, she hadn't the heart to let him down. 'All right, but you owe me one. Give me a minute to make myself presentable and I'll be up there.' She reached into a drawer for her bag, and rose. 'Who is it, do you know?'

He paused briefly on his way out. 'Ben Radford, the merchant banker. Not someone you'd want to upset. Thanks, Kay; Matthew shouldn't be more than half an hour.'

With a wave of his hand he disappeared, not realising he'd left Kay in a state of shock. Ben Radford! His name was a silent groan. Of all the pieces of bad luck. If she'd known she never would have agreed. Now she was committed to spending at least thirty minutes in his unenviable company. She didn't know what she'd done to deserve it, but it was too late to back out.

Hurrying to the ladies' washroom, she surveyed her face. Was it any wonder she looked pale? But that was soon remedied with make-up. Unfortunately there was nothing she could do about her black pencil skirt and tailored white blouse, which were comfortable but quite definitely prissy. Then immediately she was annoyed at herself for allowing just his name to put her into a spin. He was just a man, for heaven's sake! Deciding she'd done enough primping, she let herself out and headed for the lift.

Kay nodded to Matthew Winterbourne's secretary as she passed through en route for his office. At the door she stopped and rather nervously smoothed her skirt down over her hips before taking a deep breath and entering. Ben Radford had his back to her, standing at the window, but he turned as he heard the door, his smile turning to a deep frown.

'Good morning,' Kay greeted politely, despite her heart's alarming tendency to gallop out of control. She then found herself the object of a long leisurely perusal from her head to her feet, the result of which clearly found her wanting, and made her blood boil.

'My, my, you do turn up in the most unexpected places,' he drawled, amusement dancing in his eyes as he witnessed her reaction. Slipping his hands into his trouser pockets, he paced towards her.

Still angered by the way he had looked her over so scathingly, it was an effort for her to remain polite, as the twitch of his lips showed he knew only too well. 'It's not unexpected at all. I happen to work here. I came to tell you that Mr Winterbourne has been delayed. An effort was made to contact you, but you couldn't be found.' Her chilly ghost of a smile suggested that any waiting he had to do was therefore his own fault.

His response to that was to step unnervingly closer to her, so that she was made vitally aware of the height and breadth of him, and the pure male scent that mingled with his cologne and so appealed to her senses that they went into overdrive.

'Meanwhile, you were sent to keep me...entertained?' he queried in a sexily husky voice.

Although she knew it was deliberate, on one level his voice did amazing things to her insides, and in pure self-defence she summoned anger. 'No, I damn well was not!' she responded, eyes spitting sparks.

His eyebrow quirked. 'Tsk, tsk, now is that any way to talk to a client?'

It was a timely reminder, and Kay fought an inner battle for control, because he was right, damn him. It was not company policy to actively antagonise clients, especially ones designated VIPs. Yet there was clearly a double standard at work here, for, while he had leave to say what he liked, she must keep her place. 'I'll have you know it wasn't my idea to come here.'

Ben Radford laughed. 'No, I can well believe that! So, you work here, do you? That's very interesting.'

She couldn't see why. 'Is it?'

He sent her a broad smile and wandered over to the desk, turning to prop himself against it, arms crossed. He was the epitome of male power, leashed for now, but ready to spring into action. 'I hope you've taken my advice to heart, Miss Napier, otherwise things could become a little awkward. For you, that is.'

Kay stiffened at the renewed threat. 'I had absolutely no intention of seeing anyone involved with the Endacotts ever again, and quite frankly I could have done without this meeting too.' Because there was a deplorable part of her that found him so devastatingly attractive that it shattered her mind!

'Rest assured, there are plenty of women whose company I would seek before yours, Miss Napier,' he retorted scathingly, making her gasp in equal degrees of shock and hurt.

But she'd rather die than let him know that he could affect her in any way, and her lips curled. 'Oh, I'm sure there are, and I can imagine the sort, too! Big flashy blondes with more chest than brains!' she sniped sarcastically, losing control of her tongue yet again.

Blue eyes became frosty. 'Perhaps. They certainly wouldn't be avaricious little gold-diggers, who dress with as much sex appeal as cold rice pudding!' Ben Radford shot back swiftly.

Kay didn't know which description hurt the most, and while she struggled to find a response she was saved the need by the door being thrust open. Matthew Winterbourne rushed in, totally oblivious to the atmos-

phere, tossing aside his briefcase and holding out a hand
to the other man.

'Sorry to keep you waiting, Ben. Traffic was at a
standstill!' he apologised.

Ben Radford shook hands. 'No problem. Miss Napier
here has been keeping me amused,' he said smoothly,
no trace of animosity in his tone, which warned Kay she
should never take this man at face value.

Matthew Winterbourne smiled vaguely in her direction. 'Has she? Thanks for holding the fort, Kay.'

From somewhere Kay dredged up a smile. 'You're
welcome,' she responded before making good her escape,
but not before she heard Ben Radford's parting sally,

'See you around.' Well, not if she saw him first! Cold
rice pudding! How dared he? He was a hateful, hateful
man, and if she never saw him again it would be much
too soon.

Unkind fate, however, saw to it that, while out of sight,
he was lamentably not out of mind. It was during her
dates with Lance that Ben Radford's ghost kept rearing
its ugly head. Try as she might—and she did try very
hard—she couldn't help but compare the two men. She
hated herself for it, because Lance always seemed to
come second—and a very poor second at that. How desperately she tried to feel something when he kissed her
goodnight, but she just couldn't. And to make it worse,
in the middle of a kiss, she'd find herself thinking he
was too short, too flabby—too unlike Bed Radford! Yet
the more she tried to think better of Lance, the more
she failed, and her nights were spent in restless self-
condemnation.

Lack of sleep made her mind dull, too, and she found,
by the end of the following week, that it was a struggle
to concentrate. Never before had her beloved mathe-
matics failed to absorb her whole attention, and it felt
like the worst kind of betrayal. Never before had she
looked forward to the weekend with quite such eagerness.

She'd give her flat a good spring-clean and wash that man out of her thoughts at the same time!

Such was her plan. She should have known better. The telephone call she received on Friday morning came as a complete surprise, and a welcome distraction from the hours of wasted work the crumpled papers on her desk represented. Expecting her secretary to answer the ring, when it continued she realised Donna was out of the office and lifted her own receiver quickly.

'Kay Napier,' she stated briskly.

'Charles Endacott here.'

Kay very nearly dropped the phone. Indeed, she replaced the papers she was juggling back on her desk with almost extreme care. 'Sir Charles?' she greeted him awkwardly after a pause of several seconds, during which her brain had gone into frantic convolutions wondering what he could possibly want, and at the same time dragging up an inimical picture of Ben Radford's stony face. 'This is a surprise.'

'I've been doing some thinking, Miss Napier. Your visit was something of a shock, but it also intrigued me. I'd very much like to talk to you again, and I was wondering if you might be free for lunch today?' The mellow tones of the old gentleman were warm in her ear.

But it was another voice that made her fingers tighten on the plastic. A cold voice which had warned her off in no uncertain terms, when advising her that just such an occasion as this might arise. Finding herself in the midst of a minefield, it behoved her to step very cautiously indeed.

'Do you think that would be wise?' she murmured diplomatically, and could almost hear his surprise.

'I can see no harm in it.'

Kay sighed. 'No,' she admitted, 'but others do. Mr Radford was quite emphatic, and I think I have to agree with him. My visit was a mistake, and perhaps it wouldn't be wise to compound it in any way.'

Sir Charles sounded amused. 'Warned you off, did he? If that isn't like him! Ben is a very good businessman. Frankly, this bank would be lost without him. But he doesn't know everything.'

'He was concerned for you,' she felt bound to point out gently. 'After all, you know nothing about me.'

'I didn't get where I am without trusting my instincts. And I can look after myself. As for not knowing you, meet me for lunch and we'll put it right. Now, what do you say? It would make an old man happy,' he wheedled skilfully.

Kay, who had sorely missed having no other relatives, melted at the gentle cajolery. After all, she told herself, what harm could it really do? Ben Radford need never know, and she *had* liked Sir Charles on sight.

'I usually have lunch between one and two,' she said by way of acceptance, and burning her boats at the same time.

'Good, good. My car will pick you up at one o'clock sharp. I look forward to seeing you again, Miss Napier,' Sir Charles declared, and rang off.

Of course, as soon as she put the phone down, she started to doubt her sanity. She was laying herself open to all sorts of accusations if Ben Radford ever found out, and it wasn't the wisest move if she wanted to put the whole of that encounter from her mind.

Yet, having given her word, she couldn't go back on it, and therefore was waiting on the pavement when the silver-grey Bentley drew up on the dot of one. It made her glad that today she was wearing her favourite French navy coat dress. Anything else wouldn't have done justice to the mode of transport!

The restaurant she was driven to turned out to be situated in a well-known gentlemen's club. Sir Charles was already seated at a table when she was shown in, and he rose courteously, offering his hand.

'Miss Napier. It was very kind of you to accede to an old man's wishes.'

'Please, call me Kay,' she invited as they sat down, and paused until a Jeeves-like waiter melted away with their order before adding, 'You make it very difficult for a person to refuse.'

Sir Charles smiled faintly. 'I apologise for using unfair tactics on you, Kay. It's a habit, I'm afraid. My grandchildren call me a wicked old blackmailer.'

Kay laughed softly. 'It sounds as if they love you. You're fortunate to have such a close family.'

'I like to think so,' he agreed and a short silence fell. Kay broke it a moment later.

'What did you want to talk to me about?'

Sir Charles paused while the waiter returned with their starter, then cleared his throat. 'As I mentioned the other day, since Kimberley disappeared there have been many attempts to extort money by people claiming to know where she was, and from children and young women claiming to be her. Naturally all were referred to the police who have the means to deal with such—frauds.

'It used to make me very angry, but time has mellowed that. Today, what I feel is a deep sadness. I no longer hope for a miracle. Which is why your story intrigued me. You're such a contradiction. Everything about you is right—your age, your colouring. Yet you want nothing, except to know you're *not* Kimberley. You came to me, guilty and distressed because you had nowhere else to turn. I feel I should have been of more help to you. I would like to think that if by chance my granddaughter is alive, and if she has troubles, there will be someone for her to turn to. So, if you still wish to, why don't you tell me exactly what it is that has so upset you?'

Kay felt more than a little choked. It was a long time since she had received such an unselfish offer. Advice without any emotional strings was exactly what she

wanted, some objectivity which she seemed unable fully
to reach herself. And considering the subject was one so
close to Sir Charles, his offer was a generous one that
she couldn't refuse.

Sir Charles listened intently while she repeated her
story, still carefully editing out any mention of the letter
and telephone call, which she had decided were malicious, made by someone with a grudge against her
mother. It wasn't, she told herself, even as if it was
necessary to the story. He nodded from time to time, as
their meal progessed, to show his understanding, and
occasionally interspersed a question. At the end, they
both sat back, sipping at their coffee.

'I can see why you suddenly had these doubts, Kay,
but I have to say I agree with you about their being mere
coincidence. If your mother had not kept a diary, it
would never have occurred to you to doubt. I expect
that if we did a survey, it would show that many red-
headed babies were born on the day Kimberley disappeared, and that quite a few of their fathers walked out
on the day the ransom was paid. You're making the facts
fit the case, but only by ignoring everything else.

'No, my dear, I think we can safely say that you can
rest assured your parents weren't kidnappers. And as
someone with a vested interest in the truth, I think you'll
trust my word, hmn?'

His smile was so kindly that Kay returned it easily.
Everything he said made so much more sense than her
own circling thoughts. Instinctively she reached out to
touch his hand. 'Oh, I do, and you've no idea how good
it makes me feel to know I was being a fool. I needed
someone to put it all into perspective.'

So engrossed had they been on their discussion that
neither had seen the new diner enter the room. They
only became aware of his approach as his shadow passed
across them, causing both to look up at once, though
their reactions differed vastly.

'Very cosy, Charles. I had no idea you were entertaining,' Ben Radford drawled.

Sir Charles laughed. 'Even an old man can have se-
crets, Ben,' he replied with bluff good humour, to Kay's
horror. She knew it was the wrong tack to take.

'So I see,' the younger man agreed, turning cold blue
eyes her way. 'Miss Napier,' he greeted with an awful
quiet that spoke volumes to her.

Kay experienced a sinking dismay. This was the last
thing she wanted to have happened, and she didn't need
a high IQ to know what interpretation he was putting
on a meeting he inevitably saw as clandestine. And as
if that weren't enough, she suffered again that instantaneous and all-encompassing awareness of him. His
hand was just within her field of vision, long-fingered
and tanned, in no way effeminate. She experienced a
clear vision of it running caressingly over pearly skin—
her skin—and felt heat rise all over her body.

Yet her voice was blessedly steady as she inclined her
head. She would not let him see what effect his presence
was having. 'Mr Radford.'

'Kay and I have been having a very interesting chat,
Ben,' Sir Charles went on, as if he couldn't sense that
the atmosphere had cooled. To Kay it was a red rag to
a bull, and the very worst thing he could say.

Ben Radford, however, smiled with feigned interest.
'I'm sure...Kay has a wealth of interesting stories to
tell. Perhaps I'll look her up some time and have a chat
myself?' There was no perhaps about it, as far as Kay
could see.

'If you're trying to make a date, Ben, do it on your
own time. Kay is my guest. Besides, she doesn't have
time to chat to you. If I don't get her back to
Winterbourne and Stonely in five minutes, she might be
out of a job.'

It was extremely unlikely, but Ben Radford didn't
know that. The thought obviously pleased him, even if

his words belied it. 'We can't have that, even though I'm sure Kay has her sights set on something higher than being a mere hireling all her life.' With which parting salvo he sauntered away to a table by the window and proceeded to ignore them.

Kay knew in her bones that she hadn't heard the last of it. Ben Radford had been paying lip-service to his partner. His true feelings were that she had ignored his warning and now woe betide her! Which thought caused her lunch to sit heavily on her stomach all afternoon.

By the time she returned to her flat that evening, she had developed a nagging headache, but as she had a date for dinner with Lance's parents she hastily swallowed some aspirin and hoped they would do the trick. It was all due to the tension produced by one man. Waiting for Ben Radford's appearance was like waiting for the axe to fall.

Making herself a snack of cheese on toast, she wished she could stop thinking about him. Just to mention his name conjured him up in her mind. Conjured up memories of his kiss, too, and how she wished she could make that vanish, never to return!

She lingered under the shower and felt better for it, and, after drying herself on a large fluffy bath sheet, donned sheer silk and lace bra and panties. Once it had seemed nothing more than an extravagant luxury that her underwear and night clothes were sinfully feminine, while her outer clothes were the ultimate in primness. Now, with the advent of Ben Radford, her wardrobe took on a hidden significance, her passionate nature concealed beneath a plain outer shell.

It was as if she had been lying to herself for years—and that made her extremely uncomfortable as she slipped on a simple black jersey dress, with its contrasting white bolero jacket. Stepping into low black pumps, to lessen her height—Lance was shorter than her and conscious of it—she checked her hair and make-up in the mirror. She was pleased with her appearance, and knew she would be approved of, but was also aware that that was due to her projecting negative sexuality. She realised she didn't like that at all.

Such ambivalent thoughts made her even more unsettled, and so did Lance's reaction to her when he arrived on the dot of seven-thirty. Not a second early or late, so that Kay had the unworthy idea he had been outside, checking his watch to make sure of the exact moment to ring the bell. Schooling her features not to show any doubt or irritation, she answered the door.

'You look very nice, Kay, as always,' he flattered, brushing his lips over her cheek.

Kay had a fleeting wish that he would sweep her off her feet instead of the customary kiss on her cheek, then mentally rapped her knuckles, knowing whose fault that thought was. Lance, with his wings of grey in his hair, and conservative grey suit, would consider it an insult to her. Besides, the disloyal thought ripped at her, being beneath his dignity.

'Mother's arranged dinner for eight. We'd better not keep her waiting,' Lance urged moments later, and Kay obediently collected her handbag.

But these unsettling thoughts didn't make for an enjoyable evening, although she did try. However, for the first time ever she allowed Mrs Young's narrow-minded statements to draw her into an argument, which left that lady in a mood of high dudgeon and Lance bad-tempered, a fact which almost had her picking an argument with him, too. Which wasn't like her at all. So that by the time they left, her relief was palpable. Lance saw her to her door, as always the perfect gentleman. Out of sorts, Kay felt the need to apologise. Unlocking the door, she turned.

'I'm sorry I was such a grouch, Lance. Put it down to a headache. Did I utterly spoil your evening?'

He wasn't to be so easily mollified, though. 'You should have told me you weren't well, instead of taking it out on Mother. We could have left hours ago,' he said testily, then, clearly feeling he'd made his point, relented. 'I won't come in. You'll be better off in bed with some hot milk.'

Irritably, Kay thought he sounded just like his mother, then retracted the awful thought and its implications. She'd always liked Lance for his consideration. 'You're right, of course. Goodnight, Lance,' she murmured.

He took her in his arms and his embrace was everything she expected—pleasurable, but unexciting, and when he let her go she felt disappointed and hated herself for it.

'I'll ring you tomorrow,' Lance promised and left, his footsteps echoing down the stairs.

'Damn,' Kay muttered, annoyed at her own ambivalence. Turning to go inside, she shot round in alarm as a scraping sound came from the shadows at the end of the landing.

'What didn't you fancy, the milk or him?' an all too familiar voice queried mockingly, and a darker shadow rose from the next flight of stairs and came towards the light from her door. Ben Radford stepped into the beam, eyes glittering in a way that set her whole system on edge. 'That was Lance, I take it?'

She chose not to answer either question. Because the shocking truth was that she hadn't wanted Lance's kiss at all, but this man's. Now here he was, tempting and taunting her with every breath he took. She didn't know who she loathed most—him or herself.

'What do you want?' she countered ungraciously, although she could guess.

His slow smile said he knew. 'To have that chat I promised. Aren't you going to invite me in?'

CHAPTER THREE

KAY'S first instinct was to shut the door in Ben Radford's face, but then she realised if she did that he would only keep on coming back until she did agree to see him. Better to get it over with now than have it looming over her head like the sword of Damocles.

'It's a little late for a social call,' she pointed out acidly, yet reluctantly stepped back and allowed him to precede her inside.

Closing the door made her feel as if she had locked herself into the cage with the tiger. She took several deep breaths before she joined him in the lounge. He seemed to grow in proportion to the room shrinking. It was impossible for her to be anything other than vitally aware of his presence. He would dominate any room, but she was determined he wouldn't dominate her. Which meant keeping some measure of control over the proceedings.

'Could we keep this short? As you obviously overheard, I have a headache.' She spoke to his back as he studied his surroundings.

He swung around then, the action smoothly graceful for all that his hands were tucked into the pockets of his trousers. He must have left his coat in his car for he was in shirt-sleeves, the cuffs tantalisingly turned back. It in no way minimised the effect of his presence—rather, it magnified it.

'An interesting love-life you two will have, what with hot milk and headaches,' he observed with lashings of irony.

To her chagrin, Kay felt her cheeks flame. 'That's none of your damn business.'

Her temper was water off a duck's back to him as he shrugged. 'Just making conversation.'

She snapped her teeth, tossing her handbag on to the couch. He was being deliberately provocative, and rising to his bait was simply playing into his hands.

'What do you want?' she repeated hardily, raising her head in time to catch him taking a long, leisurely perusal of her from head to toe. It was as if he had actually touched her physically. As her nerves jolted into vibrant life, a tiny betraying gasp left her lips.

Which brought his eyes to them in an instant. 'Some coffee would be nice. I've been waiting for hours.'

It was stunning the way her lips tingled as if he had stroked them. Her immediate response was to fly off the handle. 'I'm not your servant! And I'm not responsible for you wasting your time on my doorstep!' she very nearly shouted, chest heaving.

Ben Radford ambled a step closer. 'You have a very short fuse, Kay Napier, and something tells me Lance isn't the man to deal with it.'

'Your opinion leaves me cold. And stop talking about Lance that way. I like him just the way he is!'

'Do you really? Wouldn't you rather he showed some hot male blood? Showed he wanted you?' he probed on regardless.

Her hands clenched into tight fists. 'I know he wants me. He doesn't have to prove it all the time.'

He shook his head. 'He's no match for you. You're fire and he's ice. You'll scare the life out of him, so that he'll never satisfy you. In the end you'll emasculate him and he'll hate you for it,' he added derisively, making her gasp in indignation.

'You're loathsome!'

He backed off thoughtfully, eyes piercing. 'Why so outraged? Do you think you want a nice, cold, sexless little marriage?'

That he should have discovered so easily the reason for her own sudden ambivalence made the need to hide it vitally important. Regaining control, she clasped her hands together. 'You have no right to say those things to me. How I choose to live my life is my affair,' she said with stolid dignity.

To her relieved surprise that brought him up short and he dragged a hand through his hair, a sign that he wasn't so cool himself. 'You're right. That wasn't why I came here. You have the uncanny knack of throwing me off my stride.' His tone said he didn't like that at all.

'Totally unintended, I assure you,' Kay snapped, and he laughed, albeit grimly.

'Now that I do believe!'

They faced each other across the room, as if battle lines had been drawn up.

'I thought you were intelligent enough to heed my warning not to contact Charles again.'

At least here, her ground was relatively firm. 'For your information, he telephoned me, not the other way around,' she pointed out.

He wasn't impressed. 'As I told you he would. I also, if you recall, told you not to see him,' he added unnecessarily as far as Kay was concerned. She remembered everything about that day far too clearly for comfort.

Instinctively she defended herself. 'I saw no harm in it.'

Ben Radford laughed drily, as if he had just won a bet with himself. 'Why should you? As far as you were concerned you had nothing to lose and everything to gain.'

He was nothing if not persistent. 'Except you're deliberately missing the point. I'm not after gain of any sort.'

'So you say,' he agreed sceptically, and Kay saw red again.

'I'm not in the habit of lying, or of having my veracity called into question, Mr Radford. Did you ask Sir Charles *why* he wanted to see me?' she challenged, and watched his lips thin.

'He told me to mind my own business,' he said shortly, and Kay could no more stop herself from grinning than she could live without breathing.

'And you didn't like that, did you?' she murmured with a certain amount of satisfied glee. It was nice to know he didn't get his own way all the time.

His fascinating blue eyes narrowed to mere slits. 'You're a dangerous woman, Kay Napier,' he pronounced tautly, and her eyes widened.

She was dangerous? The only one posing a threat was him, and not along the lines he meant, either. A line of reasoning she must keep him from at all costs. 'Oh, come on! This is ridiculous. You're tilting at windmills!' she gibed, and couldn't withhold a shiver at the look he gave her.

'I'm glad you find it amusing. Perhaps you'll also find it amusing to be out of a job,' he drawled icily.

Kay froze, all humour dying rapidly. 'What do you mean?' she asked sharply.

Having caught her attention, he didn't leave her dangling for long. 'It just so happens that Matthew Winterbourne and my father were in the army together. A word in his ear and I doubt that you'd be employed there for very much longer. No financial institution would want their name connected with that of an attempted extortionist.'

Without looking in the mirror, Kay knew her colour had vanished. 'You wouldn't dare!'

'Try me and see. All you have to do is continue to defy me.'

It was unbelievable, and she absolutely refused to kowtow. 'Of all the hypocrites! I don't know how you

have the nerve! What you're threatening is as bad as
what you're accusing me of!'

Ben Radford remained unperturbed. 'I did warn you
you wouldn't like it if you crossed me.'

She slapped a hand helplessly against her thigh. 'I
don't believe this! I've done nothing wrong. Nothing,'
she denied with total disbelief. She knew he could do
what he said, or he wouldn't have said it, and the implications this would have on her life. The reverbera-
tions of such a dismissal would spread like ripples on a
pond. It was blatant manipulation and she despised him
for it. 'I won't let you do this. I won't let you run my
life because of your own misconceptions. I'll say it again,
and I'll keep on saying it. I've done nothing wrong.'

She was batting her head against a brick wall, for his
expression didn't soften one iota. 'Obviously we see
things differently. However, I'm hoping that from today
we can begin to see eye to eye. All you have to do is sign
this document, agreeing never to see Charles again, and
renouncing all claim to being Kimberley Endacott.' From
his shirt pocket he produced a folded sheet of paper
which he held out to her.

Kay eyed it as if it were a snake ready to bite her. 'I'll
do no such thing.'

If a stony face could harden, his did. 'So, now we see
you in your true colours at last,' he scorned nastily. 'You
just can't wave bye-bye to all that money, can you?'

Dear heaven, how she was coming to hate him. 'You
have an evil mind. What I'm refusing to do is put my
name to a paper renouncing a claim I'm not even
making!'

'What difference does it make, if that's true?' he
countered silkily.

Kay crossed her arms, sure of her ground now. 'The
minute I sign that paper, it's tantamount to admitting I
was claiming to be Kimberley Endacott. No way am I

signing. I've told you what I was doing. If my word isn't good enough for you, then that's just too bad!'

Without saying a word, he folded the paper and put it away. Only then did he look at her. 'You're making a very grave mistake.'

Stubbornly she raised her chin. 'I refuse to tell a lie because of your inability to accept the truth,' she said doggedly, even though she knew it was a Pyrrhic victory.

His tantalising lips curled. 'The truth being you only wanted to prove you *weren't* Kimberley? Who in their right mind would believe that? Believe that you'd turn your back on a possible fortune?'

Kay shook her head. 'Is that how you see everything—in terms of money? You've been mixing with the wrong people too long. I feel sorry for you.'

Fury ripped his face apart. 'If I wanted pity from anyone, it certainly wouldn't be you! You've chosen your path and you're going to regret it. I'm sick and tired of watching people like you prey on the grief of people like the Endacotts. I suggest you start looking for another job,' he finished cuttingly and turned towards the door.

Kay watched him take two steps, torn by the knowledge that if she let him go through that door he would have won. Although she hated being manipulated, she couldn't just give in without a fight. Quite literally, her whole future depended on this moment. There had to be some other way!

'Wait!'

Her command had him swinging slowly round, eyes narrowed and watchful. 'Well? Changed your mind?'

Her brain working like fury, she shook her head negatively. 'Not about signing that paper, no.' A vague idea floated nebulously and she grabbed at it like a lifeline. 'Listen. There's only one way to resolve this. You won't believe me but even you will believe the facts if you can see them in black and white. I want you to prove I'm *not* Kimberley Endacott!'

He looked at her as if she'd gone mad. 'What trick are you trying to pull now?'

To hold on to a hair-trigger temper, Kay paced away a step or two before facing him again. 'This is no trick. Despite what you think, we agree on one thing. Neither of us wants me to be her—so all you have to do is prove I'm not.'

After a fraught moment, Ben Radford dropped his head thoughtfully and ran a hand around his neck. Kay watched him, knowing this was her last chance. When he glanced up, his eyes lanced through her. 'And at the end of the day, when I prove you're not, you'll sign a paper confirming the fact?' he demanded.

'Absolutely,' she agreed, heart beating fast.

Again those eyes quartered her, as if he could penetrate her skull and see everything she was thinking. 'All right,' he conceded at last, 'I'll do it, and there'll be no reneging by either of us, understood?'

'I'll be waiting with bated breath for your results.' She managed to instil a worthy note of sarcasm into her comeback.

In reply, he shook his head, his smile tight. 'You'll be waiting for nothing. You'll be with me every step of the way.'

She shied away from the idea violently. She wasn't a masochist! 'Isn't that taking this paranoia too far? I doubt very much if St Catherine's will connive with you in falsifying documents. I promise to take *your* word,' she argued with pointed mockery.

'If I was going there, I'd agree with you, but I'm not. I'm going to follow your roots. There will be someone, somewhere, who knows you,' he informed her sardonically.

While the idea had its merits, and normally would have intrigued her and made her want to go, the fact that *he* would be there made it impossible even to contemplate.

It would be like accepting a dinner invitation from the Borgias. A reckless, not to say self-destructive, move.

Which made her reply short. 'I still say you don't need me for that.'

He acknowledged the truth of that with a nod. 'I don't, but if you imagine for one moment I'm leaving the field open to you while I'm away you're wrong. I don't want you out of my sight. I want to know where you are at all times. I'm not giving you the opportunity to prey on Charles's kindness.'

She didn't know why that should hurt so much, but it did. She could easily have told him that she and Sir Charles had made no plans to meet again, but she knew from experience that any such protestation would fall on deaf ears. Which meant, as he was giving her no option, she had to go. The thought of spending so much time in his company left a cold lump in her stomach, and perversely sent a chill up her spine. She wished she could say it was from fear, but knew it wasn't. That part of her she couldn't control responded positively to an idea her brain deplored. Yet go she must, or there would be no end to it. She only wished she didn't feel in her bones that she was about to make a very big mistake.

'I can see I have no choice. Nothing else will satisfy you, will it? But at least I'll be there to see your face when I sign your damn paper. That will be worth everything,' Kay snapped furiously, and took a deep breath. 'All right, I'm sure you have a plan. Where do we start?'

Clearly he found her attitude amusing, now that he had got his own way. 'Is there a better place than at the beginning? Where were you born?'

'According to my birth certificate, I was born in Alnwick,' she stated flatly, and frowned when his attention sharpened.

'Alnwick?' he growled, stiffening. 'That's little more than a stone's throw from the Endacotts' family home!' As her eyes widened in shock, his lip curled. 'Are you going to insist you didn't know?' he queried contemptuously.

That stung. 'Of course I didn't know. Like a lot of people, my geography of England is sketchy at best, and of the North practically non-existent,' she protested, while her mind reeled at this latest blow. 'But it hardly matters what I say, does it? Or that to me the place of my birth was just an address on a piece of paper? All I've ever known is London. I'm a Londoner, Mr Radford.' She could have saved herself the breath.

He stepped closer, one hand raised accusingly. 'You are altogether too plausible, too smooth. There's always an answer to cause doubt.'

'Except in your case,' she intoned bitterly.

'Except in my case,' he agreed. 'I doubt the doubt. You've got to get up very early in the morning to catch me napping. I don't see that happening. I think you like your creature comforts too much.'

Her eyes flashed at the taunt. 'You know nothing about me, yet you constantly jump to conclusions. You believe them rather than the truth!'

A slow smile curved his mouth into a distractingly attractive line. 'That's because you and the truth have only a nodding acquaintance.'

Her head went back. 'While you have a direct line to it? That's some conceit, Mr Radford!' she scorned.

'The truth, as they say, will out. Meanwhile, as it seems inevitable that we're going to be spending some considerable time together, it will be better if we dispensed with formality. You'll call me Ben, I'll call you Kay.'

As Kay intended to keep the time they spent together to the absolute minimum, she didn't see the need. Besides, to think of him as Mr Radford was altogether different from calling him Ben. That brought with it a sense of intimacy she could do without. Yet she knew she'd have about as much chance of winning an ar-

gument over it as she had any other during their brief
acquaintance.

'If you think it's necessary,' she said shortly.

He glanced across at her mockingly. 'Oh, I do. You
know, we'll get along much better if you stop fighting
me.'

'We'd get along even better if you started believing
me,' she retorted pungently, and found herself on the
end of an old-fashioned look.

'My mother didn't raise any fools. You'd do well to
remember it,' was his immediate comeback. 'OK, let's
make plans. I don't want this to take any longer than it
has to. Fortunately it's the weekend tomorrow. That gives
us two days. It's a long drive, so we need to start out
early. I'll call for you at six tomorrow morning. Any
objections?'

She had plenty, but what was the point of voicing them
when he would only ride roughshod over them? It didn't
occur to him that she might have had plans for the next
two days. Fortunately Lance had promised to take his
mother to visit his grandparents, so she wouldn't be
seeing him, and if she wasn't in when he called she
doubted he'd raise an alarm.

'I'll be ready.'

He nodded. 'Good. You'd better not tell anyone where
we're going or why. This is private business between us,
understood?'

Kay folded her arms. 'Why should I tell anyone?
Besides, you're forgetting that I'm on your side. We're
the good guys. We wear white hats.'

Reluctant amusement softened his expression for a
moment. 'Right now, yours is a muddy shade of grey.'

'That's because your blinkers are blinding you.'

He grunted and glanced at his watch. 'That remains
to be seen. I'd better be off. I was supposed to be meeting
someone half an hour ago.'

Kay was dismayed to feel her insides clench up. 'Doesn't she like to be kept waiting?' she jeered acidly, and flinched at the taint of jealousy on her wayward tongue. Dear heaven, no! She didn't even know if it *was* a woman he was due to meet.

Ben Radford's smile was suddenly wickedness itself. 'Nita would wait half the night if necessary.'

So, it was a woman! 'What it is to be rich and handsome. I don't suppose it's ever occurred to you to doubt *her* motives?'

His smile broadened. 'I know her motives. Don't start criticising someone you don't know, Kay. I might begin to think you're jealous.'

That virtual bull's-eye made her pale. 'It will be a cold day in hell before that ever happens,' she clipped out, then couldn't resist adding, 'Anyway, who are you to talk about criticising a stranger? You're doing it to me. What makes Nita so special?'

He closed on her so smoothly that she didn't have time to move, nor avoid the fingers that moulded her chin. 'Because while her passions are earthy, they're also honest.'

Kay's nerves danced violently, but not at his words. It was as if she had been touched by a live wire, and her lashes fluttered down to hide her reaction. I don't want to feel this! Don't make me feel this! she pleaded silently. Not for a man who despises me! She tried to fight gamely.

'I hope she's the trusting sort. Or aren't you going to tell her who you'll be with this weekend?'

'Nita doesn't own me, nor I her. No woman will ever own me. As soon as a woman becomes possessive, that's the end of the affair.'

She shivered at the coldness in his voice, and would have moved away, but when she looked up she caught an expression in his eyes that kept her frozen to the spot. It was almost shock, certainly surprise. Something crackled on the air. She felt every one of his fingers as a point of tingling heat. A warmth that spread down and out when, unconsciously, those same fingers began to stroke gently over her skin. And in response she felt her breasts peak so that her nipples were hard points outlined against the soft material of her dress.

'Your skin is soft, like velvet,' he murmured in a taut voice, and she trembled at the sound of it. Whatever she felt, it was a shock to realise he was feeling some of it too. A shock that breached fragile defences. For a moment she floundered, then alarm bells went off. How could she forget everything that had happened?

Breathing raggedly, she tried to jerk herself away but failed. Desperately she sought freedom another way. 'Would Nita approve of you touching me like this?' The question issued forth with dismaying shakiness.

He laughed, a low sound that sent shivers up her spine. 'I doubt it,' he confessed as his eyes searched hers. 'Have you been wondering too?'

Her heart stopped. 'Wondering?'

There was a sensual softness to his intensely male mouth. 'Would the same thing happen if I kissed you again?'

Her eyes dilated. 'No!'

'Liar!' he came back swiftly, huskily. 'You've thought of little else—just like me.'

That knowledge made the muscles of her stomach clench. 'I want you to go,' she ordered shakily.

'I will, but first—we have to know, don't we?'

Her eyes widened as he linked their need, then dropped to his lips helplessly. He was right. She had to know, God help her. Had it just been a trick—a result of the tension—or would that magic still be there?

And so she offered no resistance as his head lowered, mouth capturing hers with a mastery that shivered across her nerves. The first touch had been enough to tell her it was all there, sparking a need to press herself closer and respond, forgetting everything save the desire to know more and more of this delight. Senses clamoured for the unknown as for a moment he urged her closer, his arms about her making her a willing prisoner.

As before, it was over much too soon. He drew back, releasing her. 'Hell, I said you were dangerous. I didn't realise how much! You're enough to distract a saint.'

Kay shivered as her blood cooled rapidly. Common sense was a much needed douche of cold water. Fearing she had revealed too much, she went on the attack. 'Which you're not, despite your holier-than-thou attitude.'

'I wouldn't want to be anything so boring. Nor, if you're honest, would you want me to be.'

His aim was too good. 'Why don't you go and practise your dubious charms on Nita? Perhaps she'll appreciate them!' Kay retorted caustically, regretting having given in to his temptation. 'I think you'd better go. We have no more to say to each other.' A suggestion she underlined by going to the front door and opening it. 'Goodnight.'

He paused in the doorway. 'Maybe touching you wasn't a wise move.' One finger flicked out to brush aside her jacket and reveal the blatant fact of her own arousal. 'But we both know you enjoyed it when I did, Kay. How are you going to square that with your conscience? Until tomorrow.' With a brief inclination of his head he walked away.

Kay didn't watch him; she was too busy slamming the door after him. It didn't help to have his parting shot echoing in her head. She shouldn't have enjoyed it. And in future she'd make sure there was no opportunity for them to come into any sort of close contact again.

The weekend loomed ahead of her like a trail full of pitfalls and traps. To spend so much time in his company was bad enough without this added menace. All she could do was think of the one positive aspect—after these forty-eight hours, she need never see him again.

CHAPTER FOUR

KAY was up and packed long before dawn on Saturday morning. Deciding what to wear for the journey had not been easy. She felt a need to state her position, to remind him this was strictly business. She finally teamed a white linen suit with a pale pink blouse and pink court shoes, in which she managed to look summery and businesslike at the same time. With her hair tied back in its usual pleat she gave an appearance of confidence and control. A front she needed, with the prospect of battling Ben Radford for the next two days.

A glance at her watch told her he would be here soon, so she quickly took a last look round for anything she might have forgotten. Her case stood waiting by the front door, and a capacious shoulder-bag held her personal items, including the diary, the few family photographs she possessed, and a set of three keys that she had found sticking out of the lining of the old case. The doorbell issued a peremptory summons just as she remembered her birth certificate.

'Just a minute,' she called out, hurrying to the side-board, mercifully discovering the document on top of the litter in the drawer. That was surely why her heart was beating a little faster as she went to answer the door. 'Sorry,' she apologised, breath constricting as she saw him leaning against the door-jamb looking vitally attractive in faded jeans, loafers and a shirt, the sleeves rolled up to reveal strong forearms. She swallowed hard as her senses reeled under an intense bombardment, and waved the offending document as if it was a magic wand and could rid her of this sensory madness she seemed to suffer every time they met. 'I nearly forgot my birth certificate. Good morning, Mr Radford.'

He pushed himself upright, quirking one eyebrow lazily. 'Ben,' he corrected, and waited.

Loath as she was to do it, there was nothing for it but to comply. '*Ben*,' she repeated, dismayed at how huskily breathless she sounded. This was what she had dreaded. Where was her resolve? She looked up to discover a lazy smile on his lips and a slumbrous warmth in the depths of his eyes.

'Mmm, I like the way you say my name, Kay, very sexy,' he murmured in a tone calculated to turn her legs to mush.

Kay felt a desperate need to drag air into her lungs. 'Don't play games!' she charged with less force than she wanted.

Ben shook his head. 'This isn't a game,' he insisted, and indeed there was a sensual softness to his expression she hadn't seen before. 'You look good, too.'

Alarm mixed with a kind of vicarious excitement, and she forgot her good intentions. 'What happened to the cold rice pudding?' she demanded to know.

He laughed huskily. 'Did that sting? Then I apologise most humbly. The truth is, last night wiped the memory of that right out of my mind. I now see you entirely differently. And believe me, I like what I see. You're very easy on the eye, Kay, even if you do seem to be dressed for the Queen's garden party..Why don't you go and slip those long, sexy legs of yours into a pair of jeans? You'll be more comfortable.'

Kay's mind reeled. What was happening here? Yesterday he'd had nothing but contempt for her; now he had unleashed a whole string of compliments. Sexy legs? Colour stormed into her cheeks and she swallowed hard. How had he managed to undermine her defences in mere minutes? She simply had to get control before this got really out of hand. 'No, thank you, I'm comfortable as I am,' she resisted staunchly.

To her dismay, he ignored her words and instead reached out to pull the pins from her hair before she could make a move to stop him, running his fingers through the long copper swath and settling it about her shoulders. '*Now* you're beginning to look comfortable. I'll wait while you change.'

Dumbfounded, Kay found herself in her bedroom without realising how she got there. Closing her eyes, she leant back against the door, trying to control her breathing. God help her, he had turned on the heat in truly devastating fashion, and she had simply melted. She had to be mad! And then to allow him to dictate what she should wear! She groaned, and on opening her eyes, found herself staring at her reflection in the mirror. There was a hectic flush to her cheeks and a bright glitter to her eyes that made her a stranger to herself. She'd never felt like this in her life—so alive, so excited...so scared!

A short tattoo sounded on the wood behind her. 'Are you ready to go? I want to beat the traffic out of the city if I can.'

Kay leapt away from the door, propelled into action. 'I'll be right with you,' she called out breathlessly, and hastily dragged the jeans from her wardrobe. She shouldn't be doing this, she told herself as she changed, but if she went out there in the same suit she had the dreadful feeling he'd personally help her change. Discretion was the better part of valour. It wasn't really giving in, because she had toyed with the idea of wearing the jeans, knowing they were comfortable.

However, when she surveyed herself in the mirror, she seemed to be all leg. The pale blue material was like a second skin. Alarmed, she was on the verge of changing and braving his displeasure when her bedroom door opened without any warning and Ben stood framed in the doorway. His blue eyes surveyed her with distinct appreciation.

'Perhaps it wasn't such a good idea after all. I can see you're going to be a distraction to my driving,' he informed her in that same lazy drawl.

All thought of changing fled, and she snatched up her discarded suit, draping it over her arm to take with her. 'If you think I'm changing again, you're mistaken,' she snapped, swerving round him and making a rapid exit, all too aware of his eyes following her.

His voice, when he spoke, trembled with laughter. 'Oh, I'll just have to grit my teeth and bear it. Besides, there are compensations. Not only have you got very sexy legs, but a sexy wiggle, too!'

Kay's temper, which had been swamped by other stronger emotions, fought its way to the surface, and she swung on him. 'Of all the disgustingly chauvinistic remarks! I'm not a sex object!' Her angry declaration faltered as she surveyed his lounging figure. With his thumbs hooked into the belt loops of his jeans, he looked easy on the eye too, and so sexy that her mouth went dry.

'Neither am I,' he answered softly, 'but you can't deny you get a kick out of looking at me, too, can you?'

Her colour fluctuated wildly. It was true, but how could she ever admit it and keep her self-respect? 'I most certainly can, and do.'

Ben shrugged. 'I could easily disprove that, but we don't have the time right now.' He eyed her small case, which he could hardly avoid, as it presented a hazard to life and limb by standing in the centre of the hall. 'Is this all?'

Thankful for a breathing-space, she nodded. 'We're only going for a weekend,' she pointed out touchily, suspecting some sort of implied criticism.

He laughed rather wryly. 'Some women I know wouldn't consider travelling with anything less than a steamer trunk of clothes. And even then they'd be complaining they had nothing to wear.'

And that was a much needed reminder of why she should never get involved with this man, never reveal how aware of him she was. There had been plenty of women in his life, and still were. She would be a fool to add herself to their number. Because all she could ever be was a momentary diversion. It was enough to chill the heated blood in her veins.

'I wouldn't have enough clothes to fill a steamer trunk. Besides, I can't be bothered to spend so much time fussing about clothes. Whatever you take, you can only wear one thing at a time.' She sounded like some prim and prissy schoolmarm, and winced inwardly at the knowledge.

It didn't surprise her that he seemed to find her amusing—a challenge he must accept. 'That's tantamount to sacrilege. However, I'd have to agree you've always looked good, whatever you've had on. In fact, I can think of only one way you could look better, and that's if you were wearing nothing at all.' To emphasise the point, he ran his eyes over her from head to toe and back again.

She stiffened, as much in alarm at what he said as in outrage at the traitorous way her body responded to that examination. It was infuriating to know her mind had no control over her physical response. Why had Ben Radford come into her life and set it on its ears? Battling him felt as though she was fighting against a rip-tide. For every stroke forward, she took two back. It left her with inanities that only seemed to make matters worse.

'You can save your dubious flattery for someone who'll appreciate it, like Nita. I'm immune,' she retorted as tartly as she could. 'Hadn't we better be going?' she reminded him.

It appeared he had time enough for a nerve-jangling response. 'For someone who professes to have no interest in me, you throw down a lot of challenges. It's a dangerous game. One day I might just take you on. I can guarantee we'd both enjoy it,' he returned, picking up her case, leaving her momentarily speechless.

She flushed angrily. 'Why are you playing this game?' she demanded, thickly.

'I've already told you it isn't a game. When I see something I want, I go after it. If that's too honest for you, perhaps you should try a little honesty yourself. Now, we're running late. So shift that delightful little behind of yours into gear, and get moving,' he suggested and turned his back on her.

Kay followed him out. Honest he had most certainly been. Too honest for comfort. He wanted her, and if he kept turning on the heat as he had today then she was in terrible danger. Because she wanted him as she had wanted no other man, and if he really tried she would be more likely to abet him than fight him, judging from past experience. Yet lying down with the enemy was one mistake she must be certain not to make. Somehow she had to build stronger defences to withstand him. If only this trip weren't so important, she'd absolutely refuse to go so much as a yard with him.

Ben's car was something of a surprise, neither the status symbol she expected nor the flashy sports car of the perennial bachelor. Instead it was a grey BMW saloon that combined comfort with power. He saw her studying it as he turned from stowing her case in the boot beside his own.

'Surprised? I don't go in for phallic symbols these days,' he drawled, opening the passenger-side door.

She sent him a withering look. 'If you're trying to shock me, you can spare yourself the effort,' she parried as she climbed in.

'Is that what you've decided I'm doing?'

She hadn't, but that didn't stop her using it now. 'It would explain your strange behaviour.'

'So, you consider flirting strange behaviour, do you?'

Kay was angrily aware that he was making her sound like a fool. 'I don't want you flirting with me!'

'I know, but hell, I've got to get some amusement out of this trip, Miss Prunes,' Ben quipped, slamming the door shut, before going round to take his own seat behind the wheel.

'Will you stop calling me that?' she ordered through gritted teeth.

He grinned, starting the engine. 'Don't like it, hmm?' he queried, eyeing her stiff figure.

Her head swivelled. 'I do not. Besides...' She broke off, about to tell him he only did it to needle her to distraction, a guess that a quick glance at his profile was enough to confirm.

'Besides?'

Kay tossed a shoulder. 'Nothing.'

He shot her an amused glance. 'Come on, I know for a fact you can do better than that.'

'All right!' she snapped, goaded into replying. 'You do it because you know it annoys me.'

Ben shook his head. 'Wrong. I do it as a reminder that underneath that maiden aunt image is a red-hot woman screaming to get out.'

Kay froze in horror at the accuracy of his claim. 'Th-that's not true!' she stammered.

'Of course it is. I'd only have to touch you to prove it. I haven't reached my age without being able to re-cognise when a woman responds to me. You go up like dynamite,' Ben argued silkily.

Lord, how she wished she were anywhere else but here. It was as if he could get inside her mind and know every-thing that was there! It was a totally terrifying concept, and one she couldn't deal with.

'If it's any consolation, you do the same to me,' he admitted huskily.

She could begin to feel herself trembling way down deep inside. 'It's not. That isn't why we're here. I suggest we concentrate only on the job in hand. That's the safest course.' By far the safest, she thought desperately. She didn't want an affair with him. She couldn't! It was unthinkable, when he thought her nothing but a gold-digger.

Ben set the car in motion before saying ruminatively, 'That's an interesting word to use—safest. Safest for whom?'

He was beginning to make her very nervous. 'Just drive. Let's not overtax your brain over a figure of speech.'

Surprisingly, he laughed. 'You have a sharp tongue, Kay. Be careful not to cut yourself on it. However, before this trip is over, I'm going to make you admit you want me every bit as much as I want you,' he advised before giving all his concentration to his driving.

In spite of the early hour, there was the usual crawl out of the city, but once they were on the motorway they soon picked up speed. Despite the fact that he drove with easy confidence, Kay remained as taut as a high-tension wire. That exchange of words had been revealing, for now she knew his intention. She had been naïve to think she could hide her awareness from him. Of course he knew how she felt. He was a man of considerable experience with women. He knew he only had to look at her to send her temperature soaring and have her behaving outrageously. Yet knowing wasn't enough. He wanted her to admit it. And if she did, what then? That was the sixty-four-thousand-dollar question.

Groaning, she rued the day she'd walked into the Radford Endacott building. Ben Radford was a far more dangerous man than she had ever expected. But she was determined to resist him, no matter what he did. He saw her as a challenge, and that was demeaning. He wanted to prove a point, and to give in under those circumstances could destroy her. It wouldn't be easy, because she would be fighting herself, too, but she'd do it. Her sense of self-worth demanded it.

At nine o'clock, Ben steered the car into a motorway service station. Until then Kay hadn't realised how thirsty she was, and she followed him into the cafeteria, which was already buzzing with noise. Not that she was complaining. Although she had eventually managed to relax, she still preferred not to be alone with him any longer than she had to. He took a quick look round. There seemed to be queues everywhere.

'I'll get the drinks; you'd better find us some seats. Coffee OK for you?' At her nod he went to join the shortest queue.

Kay managed to find a free table by a window, but it was some time before he joined her, bearing a tray on which sat two cups of coffee and two jam doughnuts.

'I thought you might be hungry, too,' he told her, catching her quick frown as he sat down.

Her stomach rumbled at the mouth-watering sight, but she bit her lip. 'I shouldn't.'

Ben stirred cream into his coffee. 'Why not?'

Kay added only a dash of cream to her own cup. 'I'm not in the habit of indulging myself——' she began, and would have gone on to add, this early in the morning, only he didn't allow her to finish.

He looked up, lips curved slightly. 'It might do you good to indulge yourself once in a while,' he murmured, and when her eyes shot to his, enlarged, 'so you don't make the wrong choices later.'

After a moment's stunned surprise, she shut her mouth with a snap. He wasn't talking about the cakes, as she very well knew. He was back to that earlier incident. She was angered by his persistence, but a moment's thought made her see it was an opportunity to shore up her defences. 'I happen to know what's good for me and what isn't,' she told him with a chilly smile. She knew she sounded hopelessly starchy, but she had to keep him at a distance at all costs.

Ben considered that a while as he chewed on a mouthful of doughnut, eyeing the oozing jam. 'Do you? Yet you could be making a big mistake by refusing to indulge this time.'

'On the contrary, to do as you're suggesting would be an even bigger mistake.'

His eyes openly flirted with her. 'There is no substitute for experience,' he countered smoothly, licking the remains of the jam from his fingers in a way that should have been innocent, yet somehow wasn't.

She hated him for toying with her this way, just because he wanted her to admit to the passion that had flared between them. He might enjoy playing his manipulative games, but she'd be damned if she'd give him the smallest satisfaction! 'You're absolutely right. I shouldn't reject it out of hand, although I'd rather it was a cream cake.' Snatching up the doughnut, she bit into it. 'Delicious! There, are you satisfied now?' There was a challenging light of battle in her eye, daring him to take it further. She should have known better.

'Not yet, but I'm working on it.' His smile was slow as he sat back, ultimately relaxed. 'So, you're a secret cream cake eater.' As slow as his smile, he allowed his eyes to run over what he could see, which was altogether too much. It raised her temperature instantly. 'I should have guessed. Everything shouts it out, yet you practise to deceive. That begs the question—why?'

My God, he was an adept at changing tack and yet still keeping right on course! She should have known he'd only come at her from a different direction. He wanted his pound of flesh, and was determined to get it. Wishing the whole subject had never come up, Kay laughed, although it held a dismaying ring of desperation. 'You really do have some wild flights of fancy, don't you? There is no deception. I am what you see.'

He tilted his head. 'Really? Would you like to know what I see? A woman who, for some reason, is determined to deny her emotions.'

Kay gasped. He had no right to say that just because she refused to do his bidding. 'If by that you mean that I won't make myself freely available to you, that I refuse to be used and exploited, then I see absolutely nothing wrong with it,' she pronounced forcefully.

His smile told her she had made another false move. 'If I really used and exploited women, should you respond to me the way you do?' he pointed out, eyes lowering speakingly to her breasts.

She didn't need to look to know what he could see; she could feel the way her nipples responded, hardening into hard, betraying points. After all she had endured, that was the outside of enough, and she went up like tinder. 'Stop looking at me like that!'

There was something altogether wolfish in his smile as he went for the kill. 'Like what? As if I could enjoy you as much as that doughnut? Your body was made for passion, and I'd be less than a man if I didn't notice it. Or want to be the one to arouse it.'

Kay had stood all she intended to. Careless of the fact that she drew a great deal of localised attention to herself, she shot to her feet. 'Well, you'd better not damn well try!' she spat at him, and stalked off between the tables as if the devil were at her heels. Which, as far as she was concerned, he was.

By the time she reached the car, she was trembling in every limb. How dared he? How dared he talk to her like that just for his own amusement? And it could only be amusement. She was nothing to him except someone he wanted out of his life as swiftly as possible. But along the way he wasn't averse to playing with her—in his bed! Mind boiling, unable to get into the vehicle, she paced up and down, stoking the fires, until footsteps alerted her to his arrival. She heard the locks click open.

'Running away won't change anything,' Ben said silkily.

Kay spun around, ready to spit nails. 'Excuse me? Did you say something?'

A flash of anger crossed his face and she could almost see him rein it in. He didn't like receiving it, only dishing it out, she thought with grim satisfaction.

'Get in the car,' he ordered shortly.

'With pleasure!' she snapped, but before she did she retrieved her jacket from the back seat and put it on. Only then did she sit down and close the door.

From his own seat, Ben sent her an amused look. 'Wearing that won't make me forget what I know is underneath.'

Kay stared stonily ahead of her. 'Then perhaps thinking of Nita will,' she said, and was compelled to look at him when he laughed.

His hand reached out, circling her throat, his fingers caressing the throbbing pulse under her skin. 'You use her name like a talisman to ward off my evil thoughts. I like crossing swords with you, Kay, you always manage to surprise me, but there's something I've discovered I enjoy doing with you more.'

In the next instant his head had dipped, his mouth finding hers in a kiss that drowned out thought. She did try to fight free, but it was always an unequal struggle—two to one. With a helpless little moan, she subsided, welcoming the invasion of his tongue, kissing him back with a mounting passion. When his lips left hers, she uttered a protesting groan, only to lose her breath as he pressed open-mouthed kisses down her throat before seeking her ear and tracing erotic patterns there with his tongue.

His breathing was erratic, and he groaned softly. 'Say it,' he urged huskily. 'I want to hear you say it, Kay.'

Sanity returned as his words filtered through, and she froze, thrusting him away. 'No!'

Sitting up, Ben eyed her through narrowed eyes. 'Why not? You tell me in everything but words every time I touch you.'

Kay found herself very near to tears. 'Maybe I do, but don't think I'm proud of it! Why in heaven's name can't you just leave me alone?'

'Because I can't fight this any more than you can,' Ben admitted harshly. 'I didn't want it, but I'm being honest about it. You should be honest with yourself, too. We want each other. There's nothing we can do about it, except accept the inevitable.'

Her eyes seemed riveted to his. 'You mean give in to it?'

He nodded. 'It won't go away until we do.'

Kay gave a hollow laugh. 'Maybe that's your answer, but it isn't mine. I'll never admit it, because while I don't it doesn't exist!'

Ben looked scornful. 'Like a child, you think if you ignore it it will just go away? You've a hell of a lot to learn, Kay.'

'Not from you! Never from you!' she rejected instantly.

A light entered his eyes that made her shiver. 'Then you'll never learn it from another man. It's my arms you come alive in, my kisses you crave!' Slowly the gleam faded and he relaxed. 'Of course, I could be wrong. Perhaps you treat all men the same.' Then he shook his head and answered his own question. 'No, I was right the first time in thinking that response was reserved for me.'

Kay felt buffeted by internal and external emotions. Her mind reeled with them. All she knew for sure was that she must continue to fight him. 'Don't flatter yourself! You're not special in any way.' But he was. That was the trouble. He'd made her come alive in a way she didn't want. She was so aware of him right now that minute that it was painful. Everything combined to overwhelm her. The scent, size and heat of him. And the devil of it was that he knew it.

Somehow…somehow she had to stop him from playing these tortuous games with her emotions. The means of doing it was chance, coming to her out of the ether.

'In fact…' She paused as a notion popped into her mind. 'In fact, you're about as special as my father. He left the same day the Endacotts paid the ransom for Kimberley,' she enlarged, and watched him freeze off. She had side-tracked him successfully.

'Another coincidence?' he drawled nastily, and she winced despite her relief.

'If I was claiming what we both know I'm not.'

'Are we?' he demanded tersely, and gave himself a shake. 'You should have kept quiet. You almost had me forgetting why we're here. I must be going soft in the head! Let's go.'

Kay breathed a silent sigh of relief, thankful to have stopped him. Thankful to be on the move again. But the reaction to what had passed wasn't over. She still trembled inside. Yet as that slowly subsided, she deplored her loss of control. Every time she rose to the bait, he won. And every victory whittled away at her control, creating a vicious circle. For her own self-protection it couldn't happen again—*must* not happen. Or something told her she might just not survive the next few days.

Alnwick Castle gleamed in the noonday sun as they arrived at their final destination. The second half of the journey had been tense, and they had scarcely exchanged half a dozen words since leaving the service stop.

Yet it was something else that had dominated Kay's thoughts for the past half-hour. She had experienced a strange sensation of coming home, although she had never been to the north of England. It was uncanny, but she knew *this* was where she belonged. Where she wanted to stay.

Jean Napier had never mentioned it at all, so naturally Kay had always believed her mother was native to the south, too. Ridiculously, even up to that moment, she hadn't fully comprehended that this country represented her mother's roots—her own roots, too. Now, though, seeing the beauty of the town, she wondered how her mother could have blanked it all out so completely.

A fresh breath of life seemed to enter her, and she felt curiously lighter of heart and spirit. Which was why, when Ben stopped the car on the outskirts of the town, she forgot all the acrimony and sighed aloud. 'Isn't it beautiful? It's crazy, I know, but...I think I've come home.' Her voice was almost an awed whisper, and she looked at him with the ghost of a smile on her lips.

Something flickered in his eyes and was gone too quickly for her to grasp it. 'You said you were a Londoner,' he reminded her repressively, but her spirit wouldn't be so easily cast down.

Breathing deeply, she looked about her. 'That's because I'd never been here.'

Ben paralleled her scrutiny but remained unmoved. 'Just wait until it rains. And there's no night-life as you're used to in the city.'

'Who said I'm used to night-life? You don't know anything about me, to make those sort of judgements.' Her smile faded away. It wasn't that at all, she realised belatedly. 'Why is it wrong for me to think I could be happy here? Because it's too close to the Endacotts? Even if I'm proved right, you wouldn't want me anywhere near them, would you? Yet I wouldn't do them any harm.'

Ben's expression became grim. 'Charles already feels some responsibility towards you. He'd take you into his extended family with all the generosity he's capable of.'

Unbidden, a lump lodged in her throat at the thought. She hadn't realised just how lonely she was, or that Lance had failed to fill any sort of gap. It was a telling moment. 'Would that be so bad?' Something ripped its way through her heart. 'Or would you resent my presence in your space?'

A muscle ticked in his jaw. 'Yes, I'm part of the family,' he concurred harshly, 'but that's not the reason. You'd be a constant reminder of what Marsha has lost. She's suffered enough without you rubbing salt into the wound.'

Kay pressed faintly trembling lips together. 'I see. And you'd make sure I had no place, wouldn't you?'

There was determination in his face despite his words. 'I couldn't stop you from living here.'

'Thanks very much! You're too gracious!' she returned sarcastically, desperate to hide a depth of hurt that rocked her to her core. 'Perhaps I should carry a bell and cry "unclean"?' She looked steadily out of the window, but Ben reached out a hand to twist her to face him.

'My loyalties were decided a long time ago. I treat all prospective threats the same,' he said bluntly.

Not quite the same, she thought cynically. She doubted if he professed to want them the way he did her! 'And what does Marsha think of all this protection?' she jeered, aware of a shaft of jealousy because nobody felt that protective about her. Refusing to accept the dart of conscience that substituted 'he didn't feel' for 'nobody felt'.

His lips thinned. 'She doesn't know and she never will. Nobody gets past me, Kay, nobody.'

Stormy eyes glared at him. 'You have no right to play God. You could be doing us both an injustice. Perhaps she would prefer to make her own decisions, and not have you shielding her.'

Ben took a deep breath, as if battling an urge to say something stronger. 'Marsha is a beautiful, fragile woman. I may have been a boy, but I remember how it nearly broke her when Kimberley was taken.'

She blinked her surprise at what that statement revealed, because he had no trace of an accent. 'You lived here?'

'I still do. Next door, if you discount the land in between,' he vouchsafed the information casually. 'So you see, Marsha Endacott was like a second mother to me.'

Her initial anger faded as she understood more fully his involvement. Yet she felt compelled to say, 'But aren't you missing the point? She survived. She had the inner strength to do that. I can understand your reasoning, but I don't believe she'll crumble so easily as you think.'

'Maybe so, but it's not a risk I'm prepared to take. I'll do the worrying, you just heed my warning.'

Kay felt herself pale. No one had ever thought of her the way this man did. Despite her resolve not to let him get at her, her fighting spirit wavered. 'Can you really see me as such a monster?' she asked, eyes enormous against her ashen cheeks. 'I walk round ants so as not to tread on them.' Her confusion was genuine.

Even so his face closed up and he stared straight ahead of him. 'As I said before, you're dangerous. Now let's stop wasting precious time. What's the address on the birth certificate?'

With a feeling bordering despair, she realised there was just no reasoning with him. She could never broach his defences even if she wanted to. Which she didn't because he was too dangerous himself—to her peace of mind and everything she had once planned for herself. The use of the past tense showed her how far she had travelled in just a short time. Automatically she reached for her bag. It was almost funny, in a painful way. He would let her into his bed, but never into his family! Well, she would do neither.

Finding the certificate, she read out the address. 'How do we locate it?'

Ben started the car again. 'Someone will have a town plan. At the library or a newsagent.'

They managed to buy one at the second shop they tried. The road they wanted meant a trip across town, through the historic town centre. The street was narrow, so Ben parked the car at one end and they walked down. Kay found her heart was thumping loudly. She wasn't sure what would happen, but her nerves began to skitter and dance.

Number seventeen had a white front door, and their knock was answered by a young woman in the later stages of pregnancy. When they explained they were trying to trace a family who used to live in the house, she shook her head.

'We only moved in two year ago ourselves. The people as had it before were called Atkins, I think. Sorry.' She did all of her talking to Ben, who returned her interest with a broad smile.

'What about your neighbours? Would they know anything?' Kay interposed, drawing a reluctant gaze. Clearly the woman didn't find pregnancy a handicap to flirting with a handsome stranger, she thought acidly.

'We...ll, you might try Auntie Annie,' she said in sudden inspiration, and once more turned to Ben. 'She's not an aunt, really, but we all call her that. She's in her eighties, but sharp as a tack. If anybody knows ought, she will. A right nosy old biddy, bless her!' she declared with obvious fondness.

Ben grinned. 'Where can we find her?'

She inclined her head to the left. 'Right down the end. The red door. You can't miss it. Happen she's out, come back and I'll make a pot of tea,' came the offer.

Kay did something then that surprised even herself. She stepped in quickly with a brilliant smile. 'Thanks, but we're on a tight schedule, I'm afraid. Come on, Ben.'

She took his arm proprietorially, and as good as marched him away.

A manoeuvre he allowed for perhaps half a dozen steps before coming to a halt. 'There was no need to be so rude, she was only being friendly,' he admonished her with a curious glitter in his blue eyes.

A glance over her shoulder showed Kay the woman had gone inside, and her smile faded abruptly. She tried to remove her arm but his free hand came out to hold hers still. The lick of flame it sent up her arm added to her bubbling temper. 'Do you flirt with every woman you meet?' she demanded disgustedly.

A brow rose speakingly at her tone. 'Jealous, sweetheart?'

Kay drew in a sharp breath. 'Hardly!' she flung the sarcasm back at him while a pang of dismay acknowledged she was lying. Because she shouldn't have been angry, only indifferent. And because that left her feeling irritated and alarmed, she went on the defensive. 'Let me tell you something, Ben Radford, you're not God's gift to women! I'd have to be crazy to be jealous about anything you did!'

Blue eyes glinted dangerously. 'Yelling at me in the middle of the street sounds like the ravings of a jealous woman to me,' he goaded with precision, and watched the result with calculation.

Her temper—as volatile as nitro-glycerine—erupted like a furiously boiling kettle. 'I am not jealous!' she hissed through her teeth. 'In fact, you leave me cold!' The lie left her lips before she could retract it, leaving her kicking herself for giving him such a perfect opening. One he was hardly likely to overlook.

His gaze narrowed speculatively on the heated animation on her face. 'Don't you just wish I did?' When her lips parted to send out a pithy retort, he silenced her with a finger over her lips. 'Ah-ah! Don't, or I might be tempted to kiss you here just to prove you wrong.'

The touch of his finger sent a shock through her system. That, combined with something uncontrollable, made her send caution to the wind. 'You wouldn't dare! Even you wouldn't make such a spectacle of yourself!'

'I warned you about throwing out your rash challenges. Now you can take the consequences!' he husked, reaching for her and hauling her against him.

Kay only had time to utter a strangled, 'Ben...no!' before his head descended, cutting off words and thought.

It wasn't the punishing kiss she expected, but a ravishment that did far more damage and drew a whimper from her throat. His lips were hot and dry, coaxing hers to part, his tongue a silken caress as it sought out the depths of her mouth, until she shivered in delicious response, melting into his solidity, aware of nothing but the sheer magic of his touch. And only then did she admit to herself that she had wanted this. That she had deliberately goaded him to it.

A realisation that sobered her instantly, and she wrenched herself away from him, sick with self-disgust. 'No!'

He hadn't tried to stop her, but there was a strange expression on his face as he stared down into hers. 'Not so cold after all.'

Kay attempted to regain some dignity, but she couldn't let that pass. 'I despise you.' But not nearly so much as she hated herself.

Ben let out a harsh bark of laughter. 'Because I took up the challenge? You did everything but throw yourself at me. You're nothing like the cool ice-maiden you'd have everyone believe.'

He knew too much—saw far too much—and how she hated him for it. Only when he answered her did she realise she'd spoken the last words aloud.

'You'd better try to keep on hating me, Kay, unless you're willing to accept the consequences.'

Nerves jangling, she swallowed hard, knowing no other defence than blank denial. 'I don't know what you mean.'

For a moment he looked almost savage. 'Sure you do. You've known it from the moment we set eyes on each other, just as I did. You've tried very hard to fool yourself but you never fooled me.'

He was telling her all the things she didn't want to hear. 'You're crazy!'

'Still the same blind, determined Kay. OK, if I'm crazy, then I'm as crazy as you. Because, like it or not, you and I recognised something in each other that day.'

She shivered, hating him for once again making her admit what she battled to deny. 'The only thing I recognised was your contempt. If there was anything else, it certainly wasn't worth noticing,' she added for good measure, determined to stick to her guns at all costs.

Ben seemed to go quite still, scarcely even breathing. 'One day you'll either go too far, or admit what lies between us.'

'Never. Not when I know how much you despise me.'

Ben's laugh was harsh. 'Sweetheart, it may come as a shock to you, but you don't have to love someone to want them. My feelings for you are split right down the middle. I might hate what you're trying to do, but that has nothing to do with wanting you.' He took a slightly ragged breath. 'OK, let's go see old Annie and get this over with.'

Kay shivered again. How could he be so cynical? For her, loving and wanting went together. She could never think of making love with someone she didn't also love, and who she knew loved her. Wasn't that the real reason she was fighting him so hard? Wasn't that why his words had struck a chill through her heart?

Hastily she shook her head, not ready yet to follow those thoughts through to their logical conclusion.

CHAPTER FIVE

THE red door was opened to them by a woman who seemed to have stepped out of another era. Old she certainly was, but of the indeterminate sort. In a long-sleeved black dress, she defied the elements. Her white hair was smoothed back into a bun, an effect which should have been prim, but a pair of sparkling, alert brown eyes gave the lie to it.

Kay took the lead this time. 'Good afternoon. We're trying to trace a family who used to live at number seventeen. We were told you might be able to help us,' she said, smiling, because somehow the woman seemed to invite it.

Folding her hands at her waist, she looked from one to the other speculatively. 'Oh, aye? And who might you be, miss?' Her manner was brisk but not offensive.

'My name is Kay Napier. It was my parents who used to live there. Do you remember them?'

The old lady regarded her with new interest. 'So, you're Jean's girl, are ye? There's not much of a likeness, but that's God's way sometimes. Come away in, I'll make us some tea.'

Obediently they followed her into a neat front parlour, where lace covers lay over the tables, and intricately embroidered antimacassars covered the chairs. There was a strong smell of lavender polish in the air, and every available surface held a plethora of knick-knacks and photographs. She invited them to sit down, refusing Kay's offer to help, and a minute later they heard her pottering about in the kitchen.

Unable to sit at ease as Ben appeared to be doing, Kay prowled about the room, and was studying the photos on the mantelpiece when their hostess returned.

'Looking at my family, are ye?' she remarked, setting the tray down. 'My Bert and me, we never had any children of our own, but I was Auntie Annie to all the lassies in the street. That's Jean on the left. She's smiling there. Happier days, they were.'

Kay picked up the picture eagerly and took it to the window. Yes, although she was much younger, she easily recognised her mother. Eloquently silent, she passed it to Ben and sat down. How much more proof did he need? It was a relief to know they had found success so quickly.

Handing out tea, Auntie Annie watched · them shrewdly. 'This your young man, is he?'

Kay's eyes met Ben's and darted away. Colour began to creep up her neck. 'No,' she denied hastily. 'Ben's just a…friend, who's helping me.' Taking a deep breath, she tried to ignore him, though she could sense his eyes on her and knew he found it all amusing. 'Did you know my parents well?' she asked with fascinated interest.

A grimness settled on those usually cheery features. 'Well enough. Jean—Jean Wollaston as was—she were a good lass. Bright as a new penny. But Ronnie, he was a trial to her.' She glanced sharply at Kay to gauge her reaction. 'I speak as I find, and if it's the truth you're after you'll get it with no frills, lass. If there was something shady going on, Ronnie was mixed up in it. A wide boy, we used to call 'em. I don't know why she stood by him all those years.'

Kay found she wasn't surprised to hear that at all. Nor was it a disillusionment, because she had no childhood memories of him. 'He left when I was a baby. I never knew him at all.'

Annie sipped her tea, nodding. 'Handsome he was, and dark as sin. No help to poor little Jean, though, but she had spirit. Only once did I see her brought low, and I worried about her something terrible. Then one day, they'd upped and left. Gone to Newcastle, I heard. What happened to her?'

Kay cleared her throat. 'When my father left us, she must have brought me down south, to London. She died a few months ago,' she explained, slightly choked still whenever she mentioned the loss.

'Well now, I'm sorry to hear that. Poor Jean,' she sighed, then reached across to pat Kay's hand. 'But I'm right pleased she had you. I told her once that a baby makes up for a lot of sadness. I'm glad she took my advice in the end. She had me that worried, I can tell you. When little Sarah died, Jean was beside herself.'

The quiet disclosure had the effect of a thunderclap. Ben, who had taken a back seat up to that point, sat up sharply. 'Who?'

Caught off-balance by the unexpectedness of their re-action, Annie blinked. 'Sarah, Jean's girl.'

Kay frowned in bewilderment. 'There has to be some mistake. You see, *I'm* Sarah. Kay was just a pet name my mother gave me,' she corrected gently, not wishing to cast doubts on the old lady's memory, though clearly it was at fault.

However, Annie was shaking her head emphatically. 'There's no mistake. Sarah was five years old when she was knocked down by a car. Jean was devastated. Ronnie, too, I'll give him that. You don't have to take my word on it. Go to the church. Her grave's there.' Sadly Annie shook her head again. 'Like a ragamuffin gypsy she was, dark like her dad. Jean worshipped her, blamed herself when she died. No, lass, you can't be Sarah.'

Kay's head reeled. Sarah was dead? She felt as if a yawning hole had opened up beneath her feet. She was sliding into it, and if she didn't quickly pull herself out, she'd disappear completely. Sarah couldn't be dead. It was too much for her to accept.

'I'm sorry, but you're wrong,' she said sharply, shooting to her feet in her agitation. 'You're mixing me up with someone else. After all,' she added pointedly, 'it was a long time ago!'

It was a grim-faced Ben who shot out a hand to grasp her wrist, squeezing it warningly, as Annie looked justifiably affronted. 'I'm sure Kay didn't mean to be rude,' he said soothingly, sending her a warning look. 'I think I can understand what must have happened, Kay. Your mother probably named you Sarah to keep the memory alive, but called you Kay.'

If what he said was supposed to help, it failed. There was no way she was going to accept anything. Because if she did... The hole loomed wider. She squared up, getting such a grip on herself that her muscles ached. 'The certificate said I was born here, in this street! Which means Annie must know me!' she declared, voice rising slightly.

'Then there's probably some other explanation!' he barked back, clearly as unsettled as she.

Annie watched them both in some concern. 'Happen one of you will tell me what's going on.'

It was left to Ben to answer, because Kay kept her lips rigidly shut. She had the awful feeling that if she opened them a scream would come out. His glance said he was ready to commit murder. 'We don't know, but we're going to find out. Whatever Kay says, there's got to be some mix-up over the birth certificate. You're quite sure Jean Napier had only the one child?' he asked, and caught her affronted look. 'I'm sorry, of course you are. You've been very... helpful.'

The old lady climbed a little stiffly to her feet as Ben urged an uptight Kay towards the door. 'Aren't you Jean's daughter, then?' she asked sharply.

At a shake from Ben, Kay got herself together, although her smile was a ghastly caricature. 'Yes, I am,' she declared firmly, but there was a distressing waver to her voice, making the statement as insubstantial as the ground beneath her dismayingly shaky legs.

Annie was no fool, as her next words showed. 'Perhaps you were adopted, and Jean didn't like to tell you. It's a touchy point, lass,' she said with kindly forthrightness.

Far too touchy a point for Kay, who resisted the idea immediately. 'If I was adopted, I'd know. It's impossible. There's a simple explanation for all this. We should never have troubled you, but thank you for the tea,' she said stiltedly, remembering her manners with an effort.

They left then, Ben striding out so that Kay had to almost trot to keep up. At his car he stopped, unlocking the door with short economical movements. Only then did he turn to her, expression bleak.

'Why didn't you just come right out and call her a downright liar? Did you get a kick out of being so damn rude?'

Her head went back, and it took every ounce of willpower she possessed to stop herself shaking. 'The woman's senile!'

Fury erupted over his face. 'There's nothing wrong with her mind, only yours. I thought you wanted to know the truth?'

Shuddering, she closed her eyes briefly. 'I do, but...'

'There are no buts! Get in the car,' he ordered shortly.

She stared at him unhappily, chewing at her lip. 'Where are we going?'

Over the roof his eyes met hers. 'The cemetery,' he replied tersely, and Kay could see he had his emotions under tight control.

She didn't want to go there. Somehow she knew that if she did everything she knew and believed would shatter. 'No!'

His fist thudded against the roof. 'If you think I'm enjoying the way this is turning out, you're wrong. The truth is at the cemetery, and you'll go there if I have to drag you!'

'God, I loathe you!'

He gritted his teeth. 'Just get in the car.'

Hating him, she did so, keeping herself as far away from him as she could. She sat in frigid silence as Ben drove the relatively short distance to the church. With extreme reluctance she walked beside him up the path. It was so peaceful that she could hear bees buzzing and birds singing in the trees that shaded the resting places. In turmoil, she had the crazy desire to reach out and touch Ben, to gain some strength and support, but he had withdrawn from her. Even if he *would* have given her the support she desired which, judging by the past few minutes, she could only doubt. Then she hastily swallowed back a hysterical laugh at the idea of asking for anything from a man she hated.

They searched methodically and found the grave they wanted after about twenty minutes. There was only a headstone, but that was enough. Kay had to force herself to read the simple inscription, and then did so three times before it sank in.

In Loving Memory of a Beloved Daughter. Sarah Jane Napier. Born 27th July 1961. Died 7th September 1966. Aged 5 Years.

It was the significance of the dates that drained all the colour from her, leaving her white and shaken, and with no option save to accept at last. 'Oh, my God!'

Ben turned to stare down at her. 'What is it?'

With trembling fingers Kay retrieved the birth certificate from her bag and thrust it at him. 'The dates, look at them,' she said in a voice so dry and husky that it hurt.

He did so in silence, then read it aloud. ' "Date of birth, 27th July 1967". Wait a minute, that can't be right. The first seven is English, but the second is Continental. Someone's altered the year from 1961 to 1967.'

Kay sank to her knees; there were tears in her eyes and she pressed her hands over her lips to keep them still. Oh, Mum, what have you done? she cried silently.

Above her, Ben was staring at the grave without really seeing it. 'Sarah Napier would have been thirty, while you're only twenty-four. She was dark, like a gypsy—while you're a strawberry blonde!' he intoned harshly.

Kay closed her eyes, racked by pain. 'Stop it!' she begged, only to feel her arm caught in a relentless grip and was pulled unceremoniously to her feet. He shook her hard, and she opened tear-washed eyes to stare at him.

'If you're not Sarah Napier, the question now is—who the hell are you?' he demanded savagely, and her eyes widened in appalled understanding.

She began to shake uncontrollably. 'No! No, I'm Kay. I'm not...I'm not...' But she couldn't say the name that hung between them like some dreadful doom.

But it was as if he couldn't stop, though he was as white as she was now. 'Kimberley disappeared in July 1967 when she was three months old, ten months after Sarah died. Annie said Jean Napier was in a bad way. That Ronnie was often on the wrong side of the law. My God, it all fits. *They* kidnapped Kimberley!'

Trembling as she was, Kay still found the strength to pull herself free. 'No! That's not true! I don't believe it!' she cried defiantly, hugging her arms about herself as if that would protect her from a truth she couldn't bear. 'How can you say that about my mother?'

'Because you've already thought it yourself. Because there,' his finger stabbed at the grave, 'lies the proof that she's not your mother at all.'

He had broken the taboo. Spoken the words she couldn't voice. She had been on a knife-edge for days now, and the result was inevitable. She broke down. Sobbing wildly, she threw herself at him, fists thudding on to his broad chest, taking him by surprise, so that for an instant he reeled back. Then he fought to capture her flailing arms, forcing them behind her back, but when even that failed to stop her, he freed one hand to slide into her hair, and brought his mouth down on hers.

Even then Kay continued to kick out, but gradually the pressure of his lips snaked into her consciousness. With a whimper, she subsided, aware only of the warmth of his mouth, the gentle strength with which he held her. Easing away, she stared up at him through stormy eyes.

'Ben?' She sounded confused, then compunction at her behaviour, and the cause of it, had her head dropping to press into his neck. 'Oh, Ben!' This time her weeping held a quiet despair.

Swearing under his breath, he swept her up into his arms and turned towards the path. 'Come on, sweetheart, I'm taking you away from here.'

Kay barely heard him. She was lost in a black despair. Totally lost. A non-person. All there was, were the tears . . . tears for Jean and Sarah, Kimberley and the Endacotts—and herself, whoever that was.

In the same state she allowed him to settle her into the car and fasten her seatbelt, but it was a long time before she became aware that they were on the move again. It was a gradual emergence as the tears ceased, and the blackness retreated to a kind of grey fog. She slept then, waking a long time later. Her head ached, and she felt deathly tired, but her mind was blessedly numb.

Glancing about her, she realised that they were driving through forest land, heading towards a sinking sun. She turned her head until she could see Ben. There was a haggardness in his profile, the skin sallow, with lines deeply etched.

'Where are we going?' Her voice sounded scratchy and her throat ached from all the tears.

Ben spared her a brief but all-encompassing glance. 'To my home. It's not much further now.'

She couldn't even summon up the energy to feel alarmed. 'Oh.'

At the wheel, Ben frowned. 'Unless you'd rather go to a hotel?'

Kay shrugged indifferently. 'I don't care where we go.' Nothing seemed to matter any more.

He shot her another glance. 'I phoned ahead. Bridie Adams, my housekeeper, is making us some dinner.'

'I'm not hungry,' she said flatly, staring out the window blindly.

Ben swore silently and succinctly, and brought the car to a swift halt on the side of the road. Switching off the engine, he released his seatbelt and turned to her, his hand on her chin bringing her to face him. 'Snap out of it!'

Her eyes slid away. 'Leave me alone.'

Tight-lipped, he released her seatbelt and caught her by the shoulders, shaking her roughly. 'I said, snap out of it!'

'Go away. Leave me alone,' she ordered dully.

'You asked for it. If you won't do it yourself, there's one way to make you,' Ben declared tersely. Dragging her unresisting form out of her seat and across his lap, he lowered his head.

At the first touch of his lips, Kay breathed in sharply. Her eyelids fluttered wildly, and she brought her hand up to his shoulder as if to push him away. Only she never did, because all her nerve-ends seemed to burst back into life. His hand, splayed out over her back, was an area of heat that spread in ripples along the length of her, while his lips... A shudder shook her as they caressed her own, his tongue a tantalising promise that teased unmercifully, ignoring her whimper of need, the begging pout of her lips, until in desperation she opened her mouth and used her own tongue in silent invitation.

He took possession then, with a deep growl of satisfaction, and Kay slid her hand up into his hair, clutching the silken strands to keep him there, lest he change his mind. Awoken to passion, she let herself drown in it gladly, her breasts swelling as she felt his hand glide to her waist, then up to the neck of her blouse, and slowly undo the buttons until he could brush the silk aside and take possession of her willing flesh. A moan escaped her throat as her nipple thrust against his palm through the thin barrier of her bra, then even that was brushed aside, and nothing could equal the pleasure as his mouth took the place of his fingers, tongue flicking out, suckling until she cried out, pressing him to her.

'Oh, God, Ben, I want you so much!'

With a deep sigh, Ben drew away from her, raising his head until their eyes locked, his fiercely triumphant, hers heavy and slumbrous. 'Say it again,' he ordered huskily.

Love-bruised lips moved to obey. 'I want...' Realisation dawned, and with a cry Kay clutched her blouse closed and struggled away from him, into her own seat. 'Oh, God!' She'd said it, and nothing now could make it unsaid. Mortified, she did up the buttons with fingers that shook.

Ben's lips twisted wryly. 'Well, at least you're back in the land of the living,' he declared, snapping on the belt and restarting the engine.

Kay flushed. 'That was a really low trick,' she condemned scathingly.

He surveyed her pink cheeks. 'Maybe, but I wasn't about to leave you floundering in a well of self-pity. I used the weapons I had. Your confession was a bonus.'

Kay refused to look at him. 'If you were any sort of a gentleman, you'd forget you heard it,' she managed to choke out.

He laughed. 'Now you've made a discovery, too. I'm no gentleman. Now fasten your seatbelt.' He followed the command by setting the car in motion again.

Kay let her head drop back against the seat and closed her eyes. His method might have been effective, but she hated him for it all the same. She spent the remainder of the journey castigating herself for a fool, and they were pulling up before a large, stone-built house before she'd had enough time to get her tattered pride into shape to face him again. Yet she need not have worried, for Ben acted as if nothing had happened when he walked round to help her alight and guide her up to the now open front door.

'Bridie,' he addressed the middle-aged woman who stood on the top step, 'this is Miss Napier. Did you get her room ready? Good, then would you show her upstairs? I think she'd like to freshen up.' Now he turned to Kay, and she was amazed to see a gentle concern in his eyes for a moment as he surveyed her. What he saw must have satisfied him, for he smiled. 'Go with Bridie, Kay. I'll be up with your bag in a moment or two.'

He had undermined her with that look, and Kay allowed herself to be shown up to a room overlooking the sprawling informal garden. The windows were thrown wide as it was still warm, and there were freshly cut flowers in a vase on the dresser. Kay sank on to the invitingly soft bed and tried to concentrate on what she was being told, but her head seemed stuffed with cotton-wool. A step outside drew her eyes to the door just as Ben appeared with her bag. It was uncanny, but at his arrival life flowed through her. He made her feel real. As if she truly existed.

Ben laid her case beside her. 'Everything all right?' The words were aimed at Kay, but he looked at his housekeeper for confirmation. She nodded, sending Kay a smile.

'Oh, yes. I was just telling Miss Napier to use the bell by the bed if there was anything she needed.'

'That's fine, Bridie.' He slid his hands into his trouser pockets. 'Shall we say dinner in half an hour?'

With a nod she went out, leaving them watching each other rather like soldiers who, now the war was over, found they were supposed to be friends with the enemy. Kay rubbed her hands up her arms, feeling chilled despite the humidity.

'I'm really not very hungry.'

'Still, you must try to eat something. You've had nothing since breakfast. Why don't you shower and change? You'll feel better. I'll come back in twenty minutes to show you down,' Ben suggested, then after a momentary hesitation, squatted down before her, taking her cold hands in his. 'Listen, this may not be the way it seems. Annie could be right about your being adopted. Your parents wouldn't be obliged to tell you. People do a lot of wrong things for what seem to be the right reasons.'

Kay swallowed hard. 'You said . . .'

'I said a lot of things,' he jumped in quickly before she could finish. 'Hell, I was as shocked as you were. But let's not get ahead of ourselves. We know nothing, not really, but we're going to find out. It means as much to me as to you now. If you *are* Kimberley, then I owe it to Marsha and Charles to find out.'

Kay uttered a little gasp as something sharp pierced her heart. Carefully, she pulled her hands free. 'Oh, I see. That's why you're being so kind to me now. I might be Kimberley Endacott. Would you care as much for plain old Kay Napier?' she asked bitterly, and watched as he shot to his full height, anger bringing colour to his cheeks.

'I'll let that pass because I know you've had a shock, but don't push it, Kay. This hasn't exactly been a red-letter day for me either. You've now got fifteen minutes. Don't think of refusing, because in the mood I'm in right now I'll carry you down to dinner if you won't walk down!'

He strode out, shutting the door carefully behind him. All the same, she flinched, and had to bite down hard on her lip to hold back fresh tears. She knew she'd been in the wrong, but she couldn't help it. Something had goaded her to it. The feeling that he was betraying her, abandoning her. Which was ridiculous, because he'd already told her where his loyalties lay. He had shown her kindness solely because he could be kind. She shouldn't have thrown it back in his face like that. It wasn't his fault that she had fallen...

No! The mental scream drew her thoughts back from the edge of the precipice. She simply couldn't cope with that now. Far easier was it to blank her mind and prepare for dinner, even though food was the very last thing she wanted.

That at least propelled her to her feet to begin the slow repair of a world that had disintegrated around her.

In the early hours of the following morning, Kay switched on the bedside lamp, threw back the bedclothes and climbed from the bed, giving up all attempts to sleep. Ever since she had lain down, her mind had been working overtime, yet all it did was go round and round in circles, getting her nowhere. As her head still throbbed dully, she padded over to the en-suite bathroom, switching on the light to inspect the contents of the cabinet. Finding some pain-killers, she swallowed two before flicking off the light again. Dejectedly, she went to stand at the window, staring out into the darkness.

The glass reflected back her almost ghost-like figure, the ankle-length concoction of ivory satin and lace making her appear ephemeral. Reflected back, too, her state of mind. She no longer knew the person she saw there although everything was intimately familiar. Her hand reached out to touch the glass. Who was this woman?

Her hand became a fist that thudded against the pane. 'Who are you?' she demanded, on the verge of desperation, but the image remained stubbornly mute.

The next instant, the stealthy sound of her door opening had her spinning round, her jangled nerves quieting when she watched Ben walk into the room, closing the door again behind him. Crossing the room silently, he offered her the glass he held.

'I heard you moving about. I thought you could use this. Hot milk and brandy. It might help you sleep,' he suggested in his low vibrant voice.

Kay uttered a ragged laugh, accepting the glass from him. 'I'll try anything right now,' she declared, taking a sip before her eyes registered the fact that he still wore the same clothes as he had at dinner, a meal so relaxed that she might even have imagined her confession in his car had never happened, if only she'd been able to forget it herself. She glanced up in surprise. 'You've not been to bed?'

Ben shrugged, running a tired hand around his neck, flexing tensed muscles. 'I've been working. My study is directly under here, that's how I heard you.'

'I'm sorry, I didn't mean to disturb you,' she apologised guiltily.

'I know, it just comes naturally to you,' he murmured, voice tinged with amusement.

Kay jolted as if she had been struck by lightning. 'What?'

A wry smile twisted his lips. 'You're not an ostrich. You know how you affect me. If I hadn't heard you walking about, then I would have found some other excuse to come up here. You surely must have known that?'

Inside her chest, Kay's heart started to thud erratically. 'No, I didn't. At dinner...'

One finger came out to trace along her jaw, and she shivered. 'At dinner I was giving you room.'

Panic fluttered in her throat. That damned confession. She had known she would have to pay for it, but not this soon. 'I need more room!'

Ben slowly shook his head. 'I've given you all I can. You arouse me too strongly. There's no way I could have stayed away forever,' he confessed huskily, coming a step closer, making her dynamically aware of everything about him.

She could feel the heat coming off him, bringing his scent with it, see the look in his eye that struck a chord deep within the core of her. Yet still she struggled, because she so much wanted to give in. 'H-how can you come here now, when I'm so confused? Do you call that fair?'

'That has nothing to do with us, and you know it, even if you refuse to admit it.'

Kay uttered a ragged laugh. 'That's easy for you to say. You don't have to look in the mirror and wonder if you've been living a lie for twenty-four years!'

Ben reached out to take her hand, drawing her closer. 'I knew who you were in twenty-four hours. The woman I want, quite desperately, and who wants me. You're tilting at windmills.' He exerted a little more pressure so that her knees collided with his. 'Stop fighting it, Kay,' he urged softly.

Something snapped inside her and she gave a crazy little laugh. 'Don't call me that! Kay doesn't exist, remember?'

An emotion resembling compassion flared in his eyes for a second. 'Hell, what's a name? You're you whatever your name is, but I'll call you Red if it will make you happier,' he declared, tightening his hold a fraction so that Kay brought up her other hand to try and prise his fingers away.

Her heart began to thump erratically. 'The only thing that will make me happy is if you...' The rest of her sentence trailed off into a startled cry as she was given a sharp tug which caught her off balance. She toppled towards Ben, and was neatly twisted so that she ended up flat on her back on the bed, with him looming over her. In the next instant, his head swooped down, his lips on hers cutting off all thought.

His kiss wasn't a punishment or a seduction, but a persistent assault that left no room for any other thought. The pressure of his lips was everything. Her instinct to struggle faded almost immediately and she forgot his hands pinned hers down on either side of her head. She subsided, and her stillness was enough to have him raise himself on to his elbows, regarding her from below hooded lids.

Breathing erratically, Kay blinked up at him, tongue tentatively exploring bruised lips. His eyes followed the movement and her breath caught in her throat. The temperature in the room suddenly soared.

'What are you doing?' She struggled to find her voice, conscious of how intimately closely they were pressed together, her nightdress being no barrier at all to the solid strength of him. He made her feel weak and yet intensely aware of herself as a woman.

'Taking the decision out of your hands. That's what you want, isn't it?' Ben explained gruffly, the warmth of the banked fires in his eyes setting her ablaze as they met hers.

Kay closed her eyes and thought she could hear her blood singing. He was so right, and that scared her, because it seemed to say he knew her better than she knew herself. She *hadn't* wanted to make the decision herself. She swallowed awkwardly as her mouth went dry.

Ben seemed to find the pulse beating frantically at the base of her throat fascinating. 'I was right, wasn't I? You've stopped fighting.' His gaze lifted, grazing her lips, her cheeks and eyes before settling on her crowning glory. 'You should always wear your hair this way. Soft and sensual. Why do you try to disguise yourself?'

Caught up in a sensuous gossamer web, her tongue peeped out to moisten her lips. It wasn't that easy to breathe now, and her breasts rose and fell rapidly. 'People don't take you seriously if you look like me,' she offered huskily, unaware of how sensual she sounded.

His laugh was low and seductive. 'Oh, Red, I'm taking you very seriously, very seriously indeed,' he declared thickly, holding her eyes so that she could see the desire he no longer troubled to hide.

It was like a lick of flame, and she sighed. 'My name is Kay.'

Releasing her wrist, he traced the outline of her lips with one fingertip. 'There, you see how easy it is. You're Kay—and I want you so badly, it's like a fire inside me,' he confessed as his lips came down on her neck, scorching her with their heat.

Helplessly she arched to that caress, weighted eyelids dropping down. 'Oh, God, can this really be happening?'

Ben groaned, tasting her with his tongue, making her shiver deliciously. 'It was inevitable.'

Her, 'Yes,' was no more than a sighing breath, yet he must have heard it, for his caress became bolder. His lips were a brand on the flesh of her shoulders as his fingers brushed the straps of her nightdress aside, revealing to his gaze the burgeoning fullness of her breasts. Kay hadn't known how much she could ache to have his mouth claim her until, through narrowed eyes, she watched his head descend. All was forgotten as he drew her into the moist cavern of his mouth, tongue flicking out to tease the erect peak until she cried out.

'Ben!' His name was broken, yet it brought his head up to hers. She thrilled at the tension in his face, the passion in his eyes that glittered wildly, and the colour high on his cheekbones.

'What you do to me,' he muttered, moving against her so that she could feel his arousal.

Her eyes widened, becoming mysteriously deep green pools. 'I didn't expect this,' she whispered, yet at the same time her hands, now free, came up to trace and mould with sensual delight the contours of his powerful shoulders.

He groaned. 'Do you think I did? I saw a woman dressed like my maiden aunt, but, my God, when I looked into those eyes!' His own eyes dropped to her mouth. 'It was as if I'd been hit by a truck! I wanted to know you—all of you. To know the taste and feel of you lying naked in my arms. To have you know me in the same way.'

She quivered at the intensity of his erotic statement. Not from fear, but because she felt it too. An overwhelming need to know everything about, and experience everything with, this man. Somehow she had always known that he could be vitally important to her. It was scary and exciting, and drew her towards realms she'd never dreamed of exploring.

'I want that too,' she admitted, and he groaned before taking her lips in a kiss that sought and got a scorching response. But even as her senses reeled, he was dragging himself away, breathing as if he'd been in a gruelling race. His fingers combed into her hair as he sent her a smouldering look. 'This is your last chance to push me away. To tell me again that you hate me,' he advised huskily.

Her blood was singing a siren-song, caught up in an exciting new world. 'That Kay doesn't exist any more.' It was true. Right this minute she was experiencing a sense of freedom, where she could be anything she wanted to be. Her inhibitions melted away, and she threaded her fingers into his hair, tugging him down to tease his lips with hers. 'Ben, I need you,' she murmured huskily, boldly stroking her tongue across his lips in a way she would never have dreamed to with any other man.

His response was immediate, taking over the initiative, probing deep into her mouth with searing sensuality, imitating the longing that started up an ache deep down inside her. She knew she had tipped him over the edge, and gloried in the sense of power it gave her. She was no longer afraid, because her fear that he would dominate her had proved groundless. In their passion they were equals.

She gave a protesting moan when he rolled away to shrug out of his shirt, then lost her breath completely when her sensitised breasts came into intimate contact with the hair-roughened skin of his chest. She arched into the delicious sensation, becoming a wild creature in his arms, shuddering at each new caress of hands and lips on her body, exulting as she felt him respond to her increasingly bold caresses of his silken torso.

Her nails scored delicately up his spine and Ben arched away from her, swearing softly as he met the feral glitter of her green eyes. His own burned in response.

'My God, I was right about you. Lance could never match you.'

Kay exulted in his statement, gasping as his head dipped again, teeth closing on her nipple, sending a shaft of pleasure through her. It was a kind of delirium, but one where everything was vividly clear. She could see his touch in her mind. So real. Where everything about her was uncertainty, this alone was real. She became lost in it willingly. Her fingers curled into his hair, pulling his head up so that she could press a string of kisses over his lips.

She could feel control slipping away, and let it. She wanted to be transported away to another universe, and moved instinctively against Ben, urging him not to stop. But the loss of control made her tongue unwary. Words came out that she had no notion of until they were uttered, and though she would have called them back, by then it was too late.

Yet, at first, she didn't realise just what she had said, she only felt the change in him. The sudden tensing of his body as he froze before pushing himself up on to his elbows.

'What did you say?' The question was one of angry disbelief.

Shuddering back to reality, Kay's eyes widened as an echo of her own voice moaning, 'Yes, Ben, yes! I love you!' returned to her. Horrified, she could only blink up at him.

'I didn't mean it. It was a mistake,' she gabbled, alarmed by the look on his face, and the knowledge that it could be true.

His face could have been carved from granite. 'You're damn right it was! Let's get one thing clear. This—thing—between us isn't love. We want each other. It's a mutual desire. A basic desire—nothing more!' he said, voice taut with anger as he rolled away and got to his feet.

Miserably, Kay watched him reach for his shirt, and was suddenly made aware of her own nakedness. She used visibly trembling hands to restore her nightdress to a state of modesty. A large lump seemed to have lodged itself in her throat and it hurt to speak round it. 'I've already said it was a mistake. I didn't know what I was saying!' she replied, sitting up slowly. How could the beauty they had been sharing have disintegrated so fast?

His eyes were like angry lasers as they turned on her. 'Didn't you? Do you make a habit of telling your lovers you love them? Maybe they want to hear it, but I don't!'

About to deny she had had any lovers, Kay bit back the words. That much he shouldn't know. He was crediting her with a sophistication she didn't have, but there was no way her pride would let her deny it. Before she could fashion a reply, he was speaking again.

'I don't need that from you. The honesty of your passion is enough. So don't start imagining yourself in love with me, Kay.'

She knew she should have been angry at his unfeeling statement, but there was something in the way he said it that made her ask instead, 'Don't you want anyone to love you?'

She could almost see him withdraw into himself. 'No.'

For some inconceivable reason, that one word sent a devastating wave of pain tearing through her. It was hard to form her next question. 'Why not?' she said huskily, and couldn't understand why her heart was beating so anxiously.

A nerve began to tic away in his jaw. 'Because I have no intention of ever loving anyone. No one, and I mean no one, is ever going to change that.'

The meaning was plain. He was warning her off. Yet she found she couldn't leave it there. 'How can you be so sure?'

His smile wasn't kind. 'Because I know I'm incapable of it. I'm doing you the honour of being honest with you, Kay.'

It was almost a physical blow, and just as painful. He was too kind! 'And how do you intend to stop some woman falling in love with you?' The question was laced with self-protective venom.

In one lithe move, Ben bent over her, tipping her head with one finger, caressing her lips with his thumb. 'I can't, but when I find out, that's it. "It's been nice, but you made a mistake, so goodbye".'

Her throat closed over. 'Just like that?'

'Exactly like that,' he concurred firmly. 'So don't go making that mistake, Kay. You see, however much your body might entice me, and however much I might regret letting you go—I'd do it.'

He would, too, she knew it in her bones. 'Then it's just as well I don't love you, isn't it?' she declared huskily, and he moved away again, once more relaxed.

'Exactly. I'd hate our affair to be over too soon.'

Already battered by elemental forces that hovered on the edge of her understanding, Kay bristled. 'We aren't having an affair!'

Ben left it until he reached the door to answer that. 'Honey, we've been having an affair since the moment we met. It's about time you realised it.' And with that telling remark he went out, closing the door quietly behind him.

Kay stared at the mute wood, wishing she had never met him, but knowing it was too late. Too late for many things. Too late to deny his parting remark. Too late to deny she had done the one thing he had just warned her not to do—fall in love with him. The truth stared her squarely in the face. Her words hadn't been a mistake, they'd been the unconscious truth. Only when she denied it had she accepted that she had fallen in love with him on sight. That moment of recognition had been that he was *the* man, the only man for her.

Yet while he might want her with all the passion he had just displayed, he didn't want her love. Despair engulfed her. What on earth was she to do? In his arms she had been her true self, and knew instinctively that she could only ever be so with him. It had to be the cruellest of jokes. She hadn't asked to feel this way, hadn't known she was capable of this depth of emotion. Then to discover Ben had ruled love out of his life was bitter indeed.

She found herself, now, faced with a choice she had never thought she would have to make. His terms left

no room for bargaining. On offer was an affair of
passion, not love—and she loved him. To keep him, she
would have to deny it, though, to hide from him the one
true gift she had. Love, to her, had always meant marriage, family, the whole thing. Could she lock that away
in her heart and accept only an affair? An affair that
would last only as long as his passion for her lasted?
Her heart said no. She wanted much more than that.
Her heart said, 'How could he know he was incapable
of loving?' Another crazy part of her said, 'Test him
out, make him prove it.' Yet another said, 'Don't. You'd
lose him quicker then, and forever.'

A groan forced its way from her aching throat. What
did she do? What did she want? Heaven for an hour—
or an eternity of emptiness?

It was too much. She scrambled beneath the covers,
switching off the light. She doubted she would sleep,
and a pained laugh left her. Ben had done what he intended, and taken her mind off her immediate worries.
Now he had given her something even more painful to
think about.

One tear slid slowly down her cheek.

CHAPTER SIX

As IT turned out, Kay must have fallen asleep somewhere around dawn from sheer exhaustion. She awoke eventually, mid-morning, feeling rather hung over. A cool shower helped restore her to somewhere approaching normal, although that was a rather nebulous state at present. She washed her hair, too, with shampoo she found in the well-stocked guest bathroom, towelling it dry and leaving it free to dry in its natural waves. It seemed pointless now to resume a disguise that had been blown. Perhaps that was why she stepped into her jeans again, although teaming them with a powder-blue blouse, and slipping white espadrilles on her feet.

Nobody was about when she ventured downstairs, so she made her way through to the back of the house. The kitchen proved to be empty, too, but through the window she caught sight of Ben stretched out on a lounger on the patio. Her eyes ate him up. She still didn't know what she was going to do, because she knew she would be hurt either way. She was hurting now, just knowing he didn't love her. If she listened to her head, then it would tell her to cut her losses now, but ridiculously there was a part of her which refused to accept that the situation was totally hopeless. Which meant she was going to do what countless other women must have done in her position—wait and see.

Turning away from the window, she found coffee warming on a hotplate and helped herself to a cup before taking a deep breath and going to join him. He glanced up at her approach. For a moment their eyes locked, and it was all there, as vividly as it had been last night.

Yet what she felt was love, and therefore forbidden, and, lest she couldn't hide it, she looked away, making a show of studying the garden.

'I helped myself to coffee. I hope that was OK,' she said, although she didn't attempt to drink any because her hand was shaking too much. The wisest thing to do was put the cup down, and she did so quickly. 'You're lucky, there's a lovely view from here.'

'You must be a mind-reader. I was just thinking that very thing myself,' Ben declared, his husky tone spiced with amusement, and she turned to find his eyes not on the view, but on her.

On cue her heart-rate increased as warm colour entered her cheeks. Not as warm as the heat in his blue eyes though, and she couldn't think of a single thing to say.

Ben's lips curved into an alluring smile. 'Aren't you going to wish me good morning?' he teased gently, and her heart flipped.

'Of course. Good morning, Ben,' she greeted obediently, wondering if she would ever be able to resist him again. That was what love did—made you feel strong and weak, helpless and invincible, all at the same time.

Pulling a matching lounger into position beside him, Ben patted it invitingly. 'You're too far away. Why don't you come over here and join me? I won't bite—unless you want me to!'

With a helpless little sigh, Kay crossed the space that separated them, but before she could sit down Ben's hand snaked out to catch her wrist, pulling her off balance, so that she landed in his lap with a little cry of surprise. For a moment his eyes gleamed down at her, then his head lowered, blotting out the sun as he kissed her with lazy thoroughness. The pleasure was swift and drugging, leaving her breathless and longing for more when he finally raised his head.

'Now *that's* the right way to say good morning,' he informed her huskily.

'I'll try to remember it,' she replied, unwittingly provocative as her tongue peeped out to probe bruised lips.

Ben groaned, and his head dipped swiftly, lips catching her tongue and drawing it into his mouth, engaging in a duel that this time left them both gasping. Resting his forehead against hers, he closed his eyes and cleared his throat. 'Bridie's gone to church. I said I'd get you your breakfast whenever you woke up.'

Lying as she was, Kay could feel the arousal of Ben's body keenly, all the more so for the commonplace conversation they were suddenly having. 'Just coffee will be fine. I don't usually eat much in the morning anyway.'

Easing away from her, his eyes brushed her with flame. 'Stop looking at me like that, Kay, or I'll do what I've been striving not to do for the past ten minutes,' he warned thickly.

She shivered deliciously. 'And that is?' she flirted openly, unable to look away.

'Hell, when you drop your guard, it's one hundred per cent, isn't it? You know damn well I want to carry you straight back to bed and drown in you.'

Now her lashes did drop. 'I thought you were angry with me after last night.'

With a sigh, Ben eased her away and on to the lounger beside him. 'I want you too much to stay angry with you for long.'

'Providing I stick to the rules?' She tried to make the question light, but failed and winced.

His hand came out and caught her chin, forcing her to meet his eyes. 'It's going to be good, Kay, I promise you.'

She tried to smile. 'Is it?'

Slowly his thumb caressed her lips. 'Oh, yes. How can we respond to each other the way we do, and it not be?'

The answer was simple—because he didn't love her. The most fantastic sex in the world meant very little without love. But that was an emotion he didn't recognise, so how could he possibly know?

Ben clearly took her silence for doubts, which, of course, they were. 'Don't back out now.'

'And how long is it going to last?'

He laughed softly. 'A month. Six months. A year. How long does anything last? There are no guarantees in this life, Kay. We have to grab happiness wherever we can find it.'

It was a knife in her heart, but how could she argue with that, when it was no more than the truth? And if, for her, happiness was an affair with Ben, then shouldn't she grab it too, and hang the consequences? She gave a shaky laugh. 'You're right.'

The light in his eyes now was one of triumph. He believed he had won. 'I know I am. I also know you won't regret it. But however much I would like to concentrate on just us, we have other business. Which is why I've been on the telephone for the past couple of hours.'

Kay dragged herself from the morass of her emotions to concentrate on what he was saying. Picking up his tone, she knew at once that something had happened. 'You know something,' she declared, swinging to face him and stretching across the gap to clasp his strong forearm. 'Tell me.'

His hand covered hers, hesitated for a moment before gently prising himself free and threading his fingers through hers. 'I remembered something old Annie said, that Jean Napier's maiden name was Wollaston. It's not a very common surname, and it occurred to me there might well be relatives in the area.'

Kay held her breath while her heart began to thud. 'And...?'

'I found a sister, Elizabeth. She's older than your mother but never married. She's agreed to see you. I said we'd call round this afternoon,' Ben disclosed, watching her reaction carefully.

She could imagine why, after her distraught behaviour yesterday. But that wasn't why she frowned. If there was more to find out, then she'd rather it was sooner than later. It was the delay she couldn't understand.

'This afternoon? Why not now? We've nothing to do.'

Ben's face unexpectedly became devoid of all expression. 'Because we've been invited to lunch, and there won't be time.'

Startled by this disclosure, she stared at him. How could they be invited when nobody knew they were here? No sooner had the question been raised, than the answer dawned. She drew in a sharp breath, lifting her eyes to his, and knowing by their reaction that her guess was right.

'Lunch? At the Endacotts'?' Alarm closed her throat for a moment. 'How could you?' she whispered finally.

He grimaced. 'Because I couldn't get out of it. Unfortunately for us, the underground system works too well here. Bridie's niece works at the Grange. As soon as Marsha knew I was here, she telephoned to invite me over as she usually does. I had to tell her you were here, and naturally she included you in the invitation.'

Kay paled, rising agitatedly to her feet. 'What did you tell her?' The possibilities horrified her. She wasn't ready to meet the Endacotts yet. She didn't know if she ever would be, whatever the circumstances.

Ben swung his feet to the ground, watching her cautiously. 'Take it easy. Do you think I like this any more than you do? I never wanted this meeting, but now it's about to happen we have to make the best of it. I told her you were the daughter of an old friend doing some research in the area. She accepted that at face value. Marsha's a very genuine person. Neither of us need mention the real reason for our being here, or the doubts we have,' he told her firmly.

Kay turned away, rubbing her fingers over temples that had begun to throb. 'I can't do it. It's impossible.'

The lounger grated against the concrete as he stood up. 'It's too late to back out.'

Her anxiety turned to frustrated anger as she flung round. 'Make some excuse. You don't seem to have any trouble lying.'

He stared back at her steadily. 'You're going, Kay, so you may as well make up your mind to it,' he told her uncompromisingly.

Her laugh was disbelieving. 'My God, but you change your tune. You won't let me within a mile of Sir Charles, but now you're taking me into his daughter-in-law's house!'

Ben's expression was inimical. 'Only because I have to, not because I want to.'

Kay crossed her arms, trying to ward off the hurt he inflicted so carelessly. He couldn't know how this attitude demeaned her. He didn't like or trust her, but he fully expected her to share his bed!

'A subtle nicety!' she retorted belligerently, then sighed, raising eyes helplessly skywards. It was all such a mess. 'I don't want to meet her, Ben. Don't make me.' Surely he could understand her position? Her parents might *not* be her parents. She might or might not be Sarah Napier or Kimberley Endacott—or some other unknown child. It was intolerable!

'We neither of us have any choice,' he told her grimly, ignoring her plea, and glanced at his watch. 'Marsha always has an early lunch on Sundays, so be ready by twelve.' He didn't wait around for her to argue, turning away to disappear into the house through a pair of french windows.

Kay hugged her arms closer around her, shivering despite the warmth of the sun. He was capable of carrying her there if she refused to go. Yet how could she tell him the main reason for her reluctance was fear? She was afraid to go. Afraid to enter a world where she didn't belong. Afraid she might feel an empathy out of a desperate need to belong somewhere.

Yet she wouldn't be honest if she didn't admit to feeling curious about Marsha Endacott. Their lives had become inextricably linked. And strangely, underlying the fear, she felt herself drawn to the other woman, wanted to know what it was that made Ben so protective of her. Wanted to know if there was anything about her that she would 'recognise'—a calling of blood to blood that could point her towards the truth.

Which was the main reason why she eventually went up to her room to change her jeans for the white suit. If it fell short of the Endacotts' standards, well, there was nothing she could do about it. They must take her as she was.

Brave words, but they did little to conquer her nervousness during the short journey. Ben was quiet too, deep in his own thoughts. She concentrated on the scenery. It was beautiful. A mixture of small forested valleys and wild moorland, which gave a sense of freedom and space, and fresh clean air.

The house they eventually drove up to had been built in the last century by someone who didn't favour the Gothic revival so popular at the time. The end product had weathered and mellowed until it blended perfectly with its surroundings. Kay loved it on sight.

Whether someone had been listening out for their arrival she didn't know, but the front door opened almost the instant the car stopped. The woman who came to the top of the steps was tall and slim, and wore her blue floral silk dress with *élan*. She was still handsome, though age had brought lines to her face, and the sunlight glinted off the faded red of her hair.

Kay caught her breath sharply, turning towards Ben for confirmation of what she already guessed.

He nodded. 'Yes, that's Marsha Endacott. Come along and I'll introduce you.' At her hesitation he sighed irritably. 'She won't bite.'

There was little Kay could do, unless she was prepared to sit in the car and make an exhibition of herself, but follow him up the steps to where the woman patiently waited.

'Ben!' She held out her hands, smiling fondly, and kissed him on both cheeks. 'How lovely to see you again. You should have let me know you were coming.'

He returned the greeting with equal warmth. 'It was a surprise visit, I'm afraid. A last-minute arrangement. Let me introduce you to Kay Napier, the young woman I told you about.'

Marsha Endacott turned, her smile wavering for a second as she gazed on Kay's hair. She recovered immediately, however, and her greeting was genuine and open as she held out her hand. 'Yes, of course, you're very welcome here, Kay. We're always pleased to see new faces, tucked away as we are out here.'

Kay, who had been staring at the older woman transfixed, jolted to attention and shook hands hastily. 'It's...very kind of you to invite me, Mrs Endacott,' she said gruffly. She saw now why Ben acted as he did. Marsha's smile was warm and welcoming but it couldn't hide the deep sadness at the backs of her eyes, nor the fragility of her slender frame. This woman had known hell, and survived—barely.

Right now she took Kay's arm and urged her forwards. 'Oh, let's not stand on ceremony, my dear. You must call me Marsha. Everybody does, except the children, of course.' She laughed lightly, without constraint. 'Ben tells me you're doing research?'

Feeling more than a little overwhelmed by all the friendliness, Kay struggled to hold up her end of the

conversation, especially with the turn it had taken. 'Oh—
er—yes. Family history, really,' she offered on the altar
of necessity.

'How fascinating. The Endacotts can trace their name
back to the reign of Elizabeth the First. There's a book
somewhere. I must show it to you.' They stepped into
the coolness of an oak-panelled hall. 'Have you had
much luck?'

Kay cast Ben a distracted look over her shoulder, but
he merely shrugged, leaving it up to her. She took a deep
breath and plunged in. 'Not really, but you never know
what will turn up.'

Marsha nodded, genuinely interested. 'I expect that's
the fun of it. Are you here just for the weekend?'

A spark of resentment at being left to fend for herself
caught Kay and she smiled. 'That's right. I wouldn't be
here now if Ben hadn't insisted on bringing me.' She
couldn't resist shooting him a sideways look. 'Of course,
I always intended to come, but I don't think he trusted
me to do the job properly on my own. He virtually
shanghaied me.'

The older woman laughed. 'You can always rely on
Ben to do something like that. He'd go out of his way
to help anybody.'

'You'll be making me blush next!' Ben growled, his
own eyes promising Kay retribution at some later date,
which sent a *frisson* through her as she anticipated the
form it would take.

'My dear Ben, you haven't blushed since you were a
teenager, and discovered girls could be fun after all!'
Marsha chided fondly. 'I'm surprised, with all that
youthful adulation, you turned out as well as you did.
By rights it should have gone to your head.'

He laughed uninhibitedly, an action that transformed
his face so that Kay could see the boy he had been. 'With
the massed ranks of the Endacott women to keep me in
order, I didn't stand a chance.'

Marsha laid a hand on his arm. 'I'll concede you the point.' Now she turned to Kay with an apologetic smile. 'My dear, would you think it too awfully rude of me to have a private word with Ben?'

'Not at all,' Kay demurred at once, though her eyes sought his questioningly, and caught his imperceptible shrug.

Marsha missed the by-play. 'We won't be more than a few minutes. Please, make yourself at home. Feel free to look around the house if you want to. We often have visitors here, so there's no need to be afraid of trespassing.'

Kay watched them disappear down a corridor and drew a deep breath. The meeting hadn't been so bad, after all. She couldn't help liking the other woman. Although, if she were honest, there was a moment when she'd wanted to be able to dislike her. However, there was nothing not to like about Marsha Endacott. She was warm, gracious and charming. Whatever sadness had been in her life, she had weathered it and allowed time to cauterise the wound. Kay admired her immensely for that. However fragile the woman looked, she had bent, not broken, under the immense strain, and that showed a strength of character given to few.

She glanced around, then, accepting the *carte blanche*, left her bag on the hall table, and took a turn about the room. It was rich with treasures, as were all the other rooms she wandered into. So different from her own home or her mother's. At least, the home of the woman she had always believed was her mother, she thought, and hated herself for that now automatic correction. Common sense said it was better not to think at all until she knew for certain.

To that end she endeavoured to fix all her interest on the house. Most of the paintings were of family ancestors and meant little to her, but there was one, at the head of the stairs, that drew her to it compellingly. She knew it immediately. There could only be one of mother and daughter. Ben had said she would never see it, but she was glad she had, for it was a masterpiece. So engrossed was she that she didn't at first realise she was no longer alone.

'I see you've found the famous portrait,' Marsha declared with a soft laugh, coming to join her and raising her hand to finger her own hair. 'They called us the Titian Beauties. Mine has faded now, unfortunately. None of us can fight age.' She reached out and touched a bright copper strand. 'I've been admiring your hair. It's a colour that does rather catch the eye, don't you think? It's the reason I was going to show you this painting, but you saved me the trouble.'

Kay started, but after a brief smile her eyes were drawn back to the portrait. The two women had been strikingly beautiful—as Marsha still was. Apart from the hair, it was about their eyes the family resemblance showed. Both had finely arched brows and a warmth of expression that mirrored gentle souls.

'Was your mother a redhead, too?' Marsha asked after a moment or two.

Kay returned to the present with a start at that particularly crucial question. 'No. Both my parents were dark. We think I must have been a throwback,' she managed to invent with admirable calm, considering the implications. She knew a wild impulse to laugh and swallowed it quickly.

'A beautiful one, in any case,' the other woman decided. 'My daughter Kimberley would have had hair that shade, too,' she added, and Kay felt her whole body lurch at the shock of the name from those lips. 'We'd planned, my husband and I, to have her portrait done with me when she grew up, but it wasn't to be.' At last she saw Kay's white face and her eyes softened. 'I see you know the story, and I've shocked you. You didn't expect me to talk about her. But I can and do. I loved her, you see, and it makes me feel better, if anything can. She existed. I refused to act as if she never had. Besides, I don't believe she is dead. I'd know, you see. I believe a mother will always know something like that.'

Kay felt a little dizzy as she floundered through her reaction. One question demanded to be uttered. She gripped her hands tightly together and kept her gaze fixed on the portrait. 'Forgive me, but…does that mean you'd know her if you met her?' she asked quietly, and held her breath, because the answer was suddenly vitally important.

'I certainly like to think so, but after all this time how can I be sure?' There was infinite sadness in that answer, yet still mixed with hope.

For her part, Kay swallowed hard on a wrenching disappointment. If Marsha had felt anything at their meeting, she would have said so, because she was as honest as the day was long. Her silence was eloquent. Whoever she, Kay, was, she wasn't Kimberley Endacott. It should have pleased her, but it just left her feeling numb. Had she really hoped Marsha would lay claim to her so that this terrible uncertainty would be over? It seemed, at least subconsciously, that she had.

Now she had to put a brave face on it, and turn to the other woman. 'I can't imagine how you survived,' she said stiltedly, her voice sounding unnatural, but seemingly only to herself.

Marsha sighed. 'In the beginning, I didn't think I would. The not knowing is the worst part. If you know someone's dead, you can grieve, but we didn't have that. Gradually, though, I developed my own philosophy. Someone once wrote it was often better to travel hopefully than to arrive. That's what I do, every day. It's kept me sane, which I needed to be for the rest of my family. Unfortunately, my husband didn't find it in him to do the same. It broke him. He was never the same until he died.'

'I admire your courage. I wish I could find Kimberley for you,' Kay declared in a muffled voice, appalled at how tragedy had followed tragedy.

Marsha Endacott favoured her with an enigmatic smile. 'Who knows? Perhaps you will. God really does move in mysterious ways. But I'm making you sad, my dear, and I didn't intend to. Come along, it's time for lunch anyway.'

Kay doubted very much if she would be able to eat a thing, but as it turned out she was wrong. The reason for that was Ben. He livened up the lunch with a subtle wit that had them all laughing. It was something of a revelation to Kay, who saw another side of his character. A side, she suspected, that he kept hidden from all but the closest of friends. Oh, she knew he would be suave enough in company, but there would always be a certain reserve which was missing now.

She found herself relaxing in a way she hadn't expected. When she had known she was coming here it had seemed as if she was entering a minefield blindfold. Now she discovered she had negotiated it without mishap. There followed bitter-sweet moments, showing her a fleeting glimpse of a world that might briefly be hers, through Ben. When, as happened frequently, he looked across at her and smiled, she knew she couldn't give him up, no matter how much it hurt.

After lunch Marsha insisted on showing them some improvements she had made to the grounds, but just as they were leaving the house she was called to the telephone.

'If that isn't the worst timing. Listen, you two go by yourselves. You know the place, Ben, down by the waterfall. I'll join you both when I can.' She urged them away, and there was little they could do, without offence, but comply.

Not that Kay was complaining. She had never felt so relaxed in Ben's company. Nor had she seen him this comfortable with her. In a mood of peaceful co-existence, they wandered side by side down through the ordered gardens to the relative wildness of the shrubbery.

'Well, was Marsha the dragon you expected?' Ben queried as they entered a leafy, shaded walk.

With her fears proved groundless, Kay smiled faintly. 'No, of course not. You didn't understand. How could you? You know who you are—I don't. Suddenly, I need to belong somewhere, but I can't allow myself to be drawn in here. If I'm not Kimberley, I have no right to be here,' she explained, with a heavy sigh. Marsha had welcomed her, but was it for herself or because she was with Ben? Because it would be so easy to fit in, for the short time that her own and Ben's lives converged, she had to be extra wary. It would end one day, and then she'd be alone again.

Ben held up a branch that drooped across the path and allowed her to pass underneath. Yet he didn't immediately release it again, and that left her trapped between his large frame and the bushes. She was forced to look up at him, steeling herself to the now almost inevitable wave of awareness and longing that gripped her.

'I'm not insensitive to your situation, you know,' he reminded her.

'But you can ignore it?' she guessed, drily, only to see that attractive curl of his lips appear.

'With about as much success as I can ignore you,' he admitted smoothly, eyes a warm caress on her face.

Kay's mouth went dry. It was uncanny. She could hear him silently calling to her. All she had to do was take a step closer. Her eyes searched his for some sign that he cared, and found only her own reflection amid the banked fires of his desire. Her breath caught as her body stirred. The pull of him was so strong, so tantalising.

She moaned, and it was his name. 'Ben.' The flames grew, his arms pulled her closer, and she was reaching up to meet his descending lips, gasping at their heat as they took hers. He kissed her with an erotic mastery that set her whole body trembling and longing for so much more, so that all she could do was press closer to his hardness as he showed her the way to that wilder shore.

When eventually he drew back, his smile was wry. 'Witch, how did you know I needed that? I don't know how you do it, but the more I have of you, the more I crave.'

Kay traced the masculinely sensual line of his lips that had the power to stir her to such depths, and caught her breath as his teeth nipped at her fingers, drawing them into his mouth and encircling them with his tongue. It was incredibly hard to form words. 'You make it sound as if I've put a spell on you.'

'You have, but you won't hear me complaining,' he agreed easily, nuzzling his lips into her palm and creating fresh havoc.

Kay sighed. 'Did you know Marsha talks about Kimberley? I wasn't expecting that. Somehow, I thought it would be taboo.'

Ben abandoned his foray reluctantly, slipping his hand down to rest on her hip as he steered her down the path. 'She's a remarkable woman,' he pronounced easily. 'When my own parents died, she took me under her wing, although I was eighteen at the time.'

Kay felt that light touch as if it was total possession, yet it felt right, for in her heart she was his. And, like all women in love, she wanted to know everything about him. 'Was your father a banker, too?'

'Naturally. It's a family bank,' Ben returned ironically.

Kay pulled a face at him. 'So you're a third-generation banker?'

They came to a fork in the path and Ben unerringly took the left one. 'Fourth. My grandfather was Charles's original partner, and they'd inherited it from their fathers. Marsha's husband Edward and my father were next. But both Edward and my father died, leaving

Charles and myself in charge,' he explained. 'Peter, Marsha's son, is still learning his trade in the States before joining us very soon now.'

Kay felt her heart contract as something occurred to her. 'But unless you want the bank to change hands you've got to have an heir pretty soon,' she pointed out hesitantly.

From slightly behind her, now that the path had narrowed slightly, Ben's reply was short. 'I'm fully aware of that.'

Kay faltered a moment, missed her footing, and would have fallen had Ben not taken swift action, sweeping her up against him. She found herself staring up into his face. 'What are you going to do?'

His grin was wolfish. 'I know what I'd like to do!' he growled, but Kay didn't laugh.

'Ben! I'm being serious.'

Setting her free, Ben stepped out into a clearing that echoed to the delicate sound of water tumbling over stones before answering. 'Get married, naturally.'

Following him into the filtered sunshine, she paled as the earth rocked under her. 'But you said you weren't going to fall in love.'

With a dry laugh, he turned. 'Don't be so naïve. I intend to marry a woman who knows exactly what I'm marrying her for. No emotional ties.'

Kay felt her throat close over. 'It sounds more like a business deal than a marriage,' she said, using scorn to hide the fact that he was tearing her heart to shreds. Had she doubted he meant what he said last night, this only confirmed it.

'Exactly.'

He sounded so clinical, she shivered. 'How horrible. So cold—and loveless!'

She had made the mistake of getting too close to him, and he easily reached out to catch her shoulders. The warmth of his touch through the thin cotton of her blouse sent her temperature rising at once. He had to know. Had to feel it too, because unconsciously his thumbs began to brush back and forth. It was as if, by touching, they completed a circuit that sent electricity flowing between them.

'Love is a much overworked word these days. Generally when someone uses it, they really mean "I want you",' he responded cynically, even as his eyes flashed out that very message.

Yet for once all it sparked off was a despairing anger. 'And who have you picked out for this lofty position— Nita?'

Blue eyes narrowed. 'It had crossed my mind.'

It almost killed her to hear him say that. 'You won't love her. Will she know that? Will she know you only want her as some sort of brood mare?'

Air hissed between his teeth as he took an angry breath. 'My God, you ask for trouble, don't you? That isn't how I see her at all. The woman will be my wife, and as that she'll have my respect.'

Something she would never have, Kay thought bitterly, and lost control of her wayward tongue, being driven on by some deeper, darker emotion. 'And how long will that keep you in her bed?' she jeered, and shivered at the way his eyes flared.

He laughed and said silkily, 'Oh, yes, I'd be worried if I were you. You just can't resist pushing to the edge, can you?'

Against her will, her eyes widened on a spiralling excitement, her pulse beating wildly in her throat. 'I don't know what you mean!' she gasped, knowing she should feel degraded by her wantonness, yet knowing she wasn't.

Ben shook his head firmly. 'Oh, yes, you do. You know your own power—your own needs and mine. You're angry for her, now, but you'll still console me when my interest in her wanes.'

Shamed colour stormed into her cheeks. 'I'd never get involved with a married man!' she snapped furiously.

His smile was mocking. 'With me you would, any time I wanted, and you know it. All I'd have to do is reach out and touch you.'

Kay gasped, but outrage was swamped by the shaming knowledge that he was right. He knew her better than she knew herself, and desperately she manufactured anger because his closeness was draining what little will-power she had left. 'You conceited oaf! Of all the despicable notions!'

'Protest as much as you like,' he laughed, 'but you know I'm right. Want me to prove it to you?'

Her heart lurched. How could he tell her what he just had and still expect her to fall into his arms? Did he think she had no self-respect? She began a desperate struggle for freedom. 'Don't you dare even try it!'

Inexorably he began to pull her closer. 'I've told you before not to dare me. I can never resist a challenge.' His voice dropped an octave as he brought her up achingly close so that she could feel the brush of his breath on her face as he stared hypnotically into her eyes. 'Or was this what you were angling for all along?'

Kay wanted to fight, but somehow she couldn't. Her legs seemed to have turned to jelly as her breathing went haywire. Could he be right? *Had* she really invited this? Had she...? The rest was lost beneath his lips. She tried to keep hers firmly closed against him, but just the feel of him set each nerve-end exploding with pleasure. The need to respond was so strong that it shocked her. Instinct urged her to open her lips and press herself against him, inviting him to take possession of what was his.

But even as his throaty growl told her she had done that very thing, his arms slipped down around her, pulling her breathlessly close. The taunting kiss had become something else, calling up and then meeting her response. It was a battle of equals. Her arms slid helplessly around his neck as she kissed him back. Reason departed. They were like people deranged—not by madness but by a passionate attraction that had the power to undermine everything.

Past, present, future had no meaning when they touched. Sensation was all. It was a dizzying roller-coaster ride that left them both breathless and shaken when at last Ben found the strength to pull away, leaving her at arm's length. His chest rose and fell as he dragged in air.

'Dear God, this can't go on. If I don't have you soon, I'll go insane!' he muttered thickly, the heat of passion lying on his cheeks. He groaned, pulling her close again, burying his lips against her neck. Her head fell back achingly, eyes closing. 'How do you get under my skin so damn fast, you intoxicating little witch? Come home with me and let's go to bed. It's what we both want,' he added as his tongue found her ear and the tip explored its shell-like convolutions.

She shivered, trying to retain a measure of sanity, though her blood cried out for the appeasement he offered. 'We can't. We've an appointment to keep, remember?'

His hands came up to frame her head as his lips plundered every centimetre of her velvety skin. 'To hell with the appointment!' he growled seductively, and she swallowed a moan.

'But you won't know who you've been making love to if we don't go,' she protested, fingers curling into his shoulders.

'Who cares?' he muttered thickly, teeth nipping at her lower lip, drawing it into his mouth.

Kay froze, the blood chilling in her veins at his callous words. He felt her withdrawal instantly, and eased away to frown down at her. She had to swallow hard to find her voice. 'I'd care. I'm not just a body, I'm a person too!' she said sickly, struggling to be free, to break the spell of his touch which could so swiftly undermine her.

Ben had to release her, dragging a hand roughly through his hair. 'Hell, I didn't mean it that way!'

Nausea churned in her stomach. 'Didn't you?'

He was angry again now. 'No, and you damn well know it.'

'No, I don't know it. Would you urge Kimberley Endacott into your bed as swiftly as Kay Napier?' she snapped back, feeling desperately close to tears.

Ben jammed his hands into his trouser pockets. 'That's a stupid question!'

Kay crossed her arms, the hot coals of desire now faded to mere embers. 'I happen to think it's a valid one.'

His face had hardened too. 'As valid questions go, ask yourself this one. Would you respond to me any differently if you were Kimberley? We want each other. We would, even if our names were Egbert and Hildegard! One day soon, you'll be in my bed. Make no mistake about it. It *will* happen,' he declared forcefully.

'And I suppose I'll have no say in the matter?' she charged angrily, hating the way he made it sound so cut and dried.

'On the contrary, the timing will be entirely up to you,' he corrected smoothly.

Slowly Kay shook her head. 'You're so sure of yourself, aren't you? It doesn't even occur to you that I'd say no.'

He looked supremely self-confident. 'Not even you can deny what's between us.'

'I wouldn't deny it, but I wouldn't have to give in to it, either,' she said, struggling not to reveal how sad his attitude made her feel.

Ben merely shrugged. 'That will be your choice. I wouldn't force you.'

Her lips twisted. 'Yet you'd try to persuade me?'

That devastatingly attractive smile reappeared. 'All's fair in love and war.'

Drawing in a pained breath, she turned away. 'Except that this isn't love,' she said coldly.

There was silence for a moment behind her, then he uttered just one terse word. 'No.'

Kay stared at her surroundings through a haze of tears, seeing the beauty of the natural waterfall and the created water garden. It was a small corner of paradise, only the serpent they had brought with them. All she wanted to do now was leave.

'Perhaps we'd better go,' she suggested, blinking away the moisture before swinging round with a tight smile on her face. 'After all, we don't want to miss that appointment.'

Ben inclined his head. 'Shakespeare had a word or two to say on the subject of names,' he countered.

'If he really *was* Shakespeare—and if he wasn't, who was he?' Kay riposted snappily, which drew a reluctant laugh from Ben. Her heart twisted. She could make him laugh, make him want her, but she couldn't make him love her.

'I'll grant you the point. Now, why don't you go ahead? I wouldn't want to be accused of leading you astray!'

Kay went, but she wasn't laughing. 'Nobody could accuse you of that. You state your intentions too clearly.'

'At least acquit me of dishonesty,' Ben argued from behind her.

Caveat emptor, she thought. Let the buyer beware. That was what it would be if she went into an affair with Ben Radford. He had been honest; everything else was done at her own risk. She wasn't a natural gambler. For that, you had to be prepared to lose. But weren't some things worth the risk? She just didn't know.

CHAPTER SEVEN

THEY met Marsha on her way out to them. If she was surprised by their sudden decision to leave, she didn't remark on it. She accepted Ben's explanation with innate good manners, coming out to wave them off, issuing Kay with an open invitation to return any time.

Kay sat beside Ben as he drove them away, in a state of emotional and mental turmoil. She had always known he could be cold-blooded, but never as much as he had just revealed. To contemplate marriage that way was awful. Not that she believed he really would expect her to be part of a *ménage à trois*; no, he had been making a point, showing her how inevitable their affair was, and that hurt. It was as if her feelings didn't matter. Well, they did, and, no matter how long it lasted, for her their relationship would be a commitment.

And in admitting that, hadn't she already made up her mind what she was going to do? Her wry smile was reflected back at her from the side window. Had there ever been any doubt, from the moment she met him? She sighed, and turned her thoughts to Marsha and the conversation they had had before lunch.

'Did you know Marsha believes she'd recognise Kimberley if she met her?' she asked, breaking the silence that had descended on them. When Ben didn't answer immediately, she looked at him, seeing the set lines of his face as he kept all his concentration on the road ahead. When he did shoot a glance her way, it was with narrowed eyes.

'So?' he said guardedly.

His manner puzzling her, a faint frown creased her brow. 'So she should have felt something when we met, if I was her daughter. Obviously she didn't—therefore, whoever I am, I can't be Kimberley Endacott,' Kay clarified for him.

'That would appear to be a logical assumption,' Ben agreed without inflexion, leaving her feeling somehow cheated.

The least he could have done was tell her not to be hasty in her judgement. But then, he still didn't want her to be Kimberley. He didn't seem to care that inside she was suffering the tortures of the damned, rocked by guilt, suspicion, anger and fear. It wasn't his life being turned upside-down, so why should he care?

The next instant, conscience-stricken, she remembered his moments of kindness. They made a liar of her self-pitying thoughts. Irritably she stared out of the window, vaguely aware they were on a road they hadn't travelled previously.

'Where exactly are we heading?'

'A village not too far away. Miss Wollaston is expecting us about four o'clock. And while we're on the subject, there's something you ought to know,' Ben replied levelly.

Her heart lurched at that. 'What do you mean?'

'Elizabeth Wollaston is a very cautious lady. She wouldn't agree to see us until I mentioned Ronald and Sarah, and even then she demanded to know what it was all about.'

There was something in his tone that warned her the crunch point was coming. 'And?' She held her breath.

'I told her I was helping you—Jean's adopted daughter—to trace her relatives,' Ben revealed flatly.

Kay's lips parted on a faint gasp. 'Why did you say I was adopted?'

His tone resembled that of an adult addressing a slightly backward child. 'Because it was easier than trying

to explain a relationship which we can't link up ourselves. Besides, her reaction was quite revealing. She was
surprised. She'd never heard of you, although Jean apparently wrote to her on a fairly regular basis.'

Kay digested that with a sinking feeling in her stomach.
'I didn't know my mother...I mean the woman... Oh,
God, this is awful! I don't even know what to call her
any more!' Her lips trembled and she pressed them
tightly together.

With a quick glance in the rear-view mirror, Ben
steered the car to the side of the road and set the brake.
He turned to her then, eyes revealing that contradictory
compassion. 'Biological or not, she was your mother.
However she came by you, she raised you, fed you and
clothed you. That can't be wiped out so easily. She'll
always by your mother, so call her that—whatever
happens,' he advised with gentleness and a degree of
understanding that surprised and warmed her.

'I know you're right. I'm just so confused,' she admitted wanly, worn out by so much emotion storming
inside her.

Ben glanced ahead at the clear blue sky. 'Something
tells me it won't last much longer. We're close, very close
to the truth.'

Kay nodded, feeling it too. 'You're right. And,
whatever the truth is, it has to be better than this, doesn't
it?'

He gave her a twisted smile before putting the car in
gear. 'I hope so. As God is my witness, I surely do hope
so.'

Elizabeth Wollaston was so much like her sister that Kay
was left momentarily speechless, leaving Ben to do the
talking as they were ushered into a very comfortable
stone-built cottage. The front parlour was neat as a pin,
and obviously kept solely for entertaining guests.

'So,' Elizabeth Wollaston said as soon as they were all seated, locking her hands across her stomach. 'You're our Jean's adopted girl, are you? She never mentioned you.' The statement was a blunt challenge, the woman declaring herself to be no fool.

Kay cleared her throat nervously, but picked up the gauntlet. 'She never mentioned you, either. If she had I would have written to tell you when she died,' she said gently.

If the news was a shock, the older woman gave no outward sign. 'I'm surprised she survived so long married to that fly-by-night Ronnie Napier,' she declared scathingly.

Had Kay had any illusions about him, they would have been shattered long ago. The consensus of opinion was pretty damning. 'I never knew him. He left when I was little,' Kay admitted rather thankfully.

Elizabeth snorted. 'Doesn't surprise me.'

'You didn't like him,' Ben interposed, although it was obvious to them all.

'I did not. I always thought our Jean could do better for herself, but she wanted him, and that was that.' Only then did her attitude soften slightly. 'What happened to her?'

'It was cancer. She hadn't been well for a long time. I have a photo of her, taken several years ago,' Kay explained, digging the small bundle from her bag and handing one over. 'You can keep it if you'd like to.'

A little colour came into the other woman's cheeks. 'Aye, I'd like that. It's funny her not telling me about you, but then, she never was the same after Sarah died. Wouldn't tell me where she was. Never gave an address for me to write back to. That was Ronnie's doing, I'll be bound.' Her tone sharpened with antipathy.

Kay clasped her hands in her lap. Annie's story had just been corroborated, without a question being asked. 'You're absolutely sure she never mentioned me? You see, I hadn't realised I was ... adopted, and I was hoping to find out more about myself.'

'Well now, there, as I say, I can't help you. But there's places you can go to now, isn't there, to find out who your real parents are?' she proposed helpfully.

It was Ben who answered. 'We're not altogether certain it was a ... legal ... adoption,' he said delicately.

'I see. Well, I can't say I'm surprised. That would be Ronnie's way, all right.' She shook her head sadly, then to their alarm suddenly cracked the heel of her palm against her forehead. 'Lizzie, Lizzie, you're getting old! I was forgetting the case,' she exclaimed in the face of their bemusement.

'Case?' Kay repeated, watching the other woman get to her feet.

'Our Jean sent it to me, from Newcastle, and asked me to keep it for her. Good lord, it's been sitting up in the spare room for over twenty years now. It'll be yours now that she's gone. Mind, you might have to break it open, young man. It was locked and I don't have the key.'

Kay felt all the hairs on her body stand to attention. 'I think I may have it,' she revealed huskily. In response to Ben's sharply questioning glance, she raised a diffident shoulder. 'I found some keys in Mum's things that didn't seem to belong to anything.'

'Jean wasn't one to throw anything away. Come away upstairs, and you can help me to find it, young man,' Elizabeth Wollaston commanded, clearly never a woman to waste time.

There was a bit of shifting to do, for the third bedroom had become more or less a store-room. They discovered it eventually, tucked away in a corner, and Ben lifted it on to the bed. Both he and Elizabeth turned towards Kay then, and she produced the keys from her bag. She singled out the third key, and it was really no surprise to her when the lock clicked open.

Kay hesitated then, her curiosity tempered by the fact that so far all their discoveries had made matters worse, not better. Yet, for all she knew, there could be nothing but a load of old clothes inside, and as she never would know unless she looked, there was only one thing to do. A swift glance at Ben drew a nod from him, and, taking a deep breath, she raised the lid.

The first thing that met their eyes was a small black book, with the word 'Diary' embossed on it in gold. Kay's legs seemed to give out all at once, and she sat down heavily on the bed. She couldn't fail to recognise the book; she had its twin in her case at Ben's house.

Elizabeth took one look at her and clucked sympathetically. 'Loved her diary, Jean did. Perhaps you'll find what you want in there. I'll leave you two alone. Come down to the parlour when you're through.'

Kay barely heard her go, for she was lifting out the book with hands that trembled. Beneath it lay a brown paper parcel tied up with string. She ignored that for a moment, opening the book and recognising at once her mother's neat hand. Like the one already in her possession, it covered a number of years, the entries haphazard. She turned to the last written entry.

... call her Sarah, but Ronnie said it was too dangerous. That's why we're leaving and going south. No one must know because he'd used an illegal adoption agency. I didn't like it, but Ronnie says we'd never get a baby any other way. He wanted me to burn the clothes she came in, but they were so lovely I couldn't. I've decided to pack them up and send them to Lizzie. I won't tell Ronnie. He's been so restless lately. I'm hoping the baby will bring us some good luck. I'll pray for it and for little Kay. I've decided to call her that because it's the initial on her clothes. I'm sorry her mother couldn't keep her, but I'll love her and care for her so she need never worry...

There was a wealth of agony in Kay's eyes as she looked up. Ben had dealt with the knotted string and was unwrapping the parcel. Her breath caught as the tiny wool and fine linen baby clothes, now slightly yellowed, were uncovered. The embroidered monogram stared up at her accusingly.

'Oh, God!' The words were a sighing moan. She watched him pick up a cardigan. 'Ronnie told her he got me from an illegal adoption agency. She called me Kay because it was on my clothes. Are they... are they Kimberley's?'

Ben had to clear his throat to answer. 'I think so... Marsha will know.'

Kay felt as if this was all happening to somebody else. Later she would realise she was suffering from shock. Right then she felt numb, her emotions frozen. Her words seemed to come from a long way away, and were spoken by a total stranger. 'So I *am* Kimberley Endacott.' It was a flat statement, for there could be little doubt of it now.

Ben looked at her sharply then, frowning, alerted by her strange tone. 'It would appear so.' He paused. 'Are you all right?'

She closed the book with controlled movements and placed it in the case on top of the clothes. 'Of course. I know now. There's no more uncertainty,' she declared flatly, closing the lid and locking it down.

Ben's frown deepened. 'Kay...' he began, only to have her head shoot up, eyes flashing dangerously.

'Kimberley! My name is Kimberley.' It sounded alien on her tongue. Alien and unwelcome. 'Kay doesn't exist. She *never* existed. She was just an initial. A cypher.' Feeling her control slipping, Kay dragged in air. 'Can we please go now?' she asked, meeting his eyes challengingly.

'Don't take it so hard,' he recommended gently.

Once more her eyes flashed a dangerous warning. She was ready to lash out at anyone, and he was nearest. 'You wouldn't say that if you had any comprehension of what it means to find you belong nowhere!'

'We know where you belong—with Marsha,' Ben pointed out softly.

She laughed, but with no real amusement. 'And what do I do? Turn up at the door and say, "Hi, Mum, I'm back. You'll never guess what's happened to me!"?'

Ben deliberately misunderstood. 'You'd be welcomed if you did. By the whole family. You have a brother and sister, too.'

Did he really believe knowing that would help? 'They're all strangers. Inhabiting a world I don't know.'

'You'll have to give yourself time to adjust. They won't remain strangers for long, and their world will become yours,' Ben replied sensibly.

'My life is in London. I work there,' she countered, feeling panicky.

Ben lost a little of his patience. 'Just yesterday you told me you felt you belonged here, that you'd come home. You can't be thinking of just turning your back and walking away?' he challenged frigidly.

Kay clasped her hands over her ears. 'I don't know what I want! I don't know what to think any more! I just want to get away from here and somehow find *me*!' Her eyes pleaded with him for understanding and saw the rigidity go out of him.

'You're right, this isn't the time or the place. I'll bring the case. You go on down and have a word with Miss Wollaston, then I'll take you home.'

'Thank you,' she said gruffly.

The old lady—Kay could no longer think of her as an aunt—came to meet them at the bottom of the stairs.

'Did you find anything to help you?'

Kay produced a weak smile. The truth would have to come out, with all its dubious implications, but not now.

'Just some baby clothes and the diary. It will take some time to read. We're taking the case with us. You did say that would be all right?' she checked hesitantly.

Elizabeth Wollaston waved a hand. 'They're of no use to me. They were your mother's, so by rights they're yours now.'

It was awful to suddenly feel you were a fraud, accepting things that you had no right to, but Kay couldn't help it. Colour washed in and out of her cheeks. All she could say was, 'If I should find anything I think she'd have wanted you to have, I'll send it to you.'

The older woman patted Kay's cheek gently. 'You're a kind child. I've no doubt our Jean was right proud of you. Won't you stay for tea?'

Kay couldn't utter a word, it was Ben who stepped into the breach. 'We'd like to, but Kay found it all a bit upsetting. I'd like to take her home.'

'Aye, I could see that. You take good care of her, young man, or you'll have her aunt to answer to! Now, off you go.'

She walked down to the gate with them, where Kay's guilt made her turn.

'I'll try to keep in touch,' she promised.

'Away with you! You've got your young man and your own life. Don't you go worrying yourself over me,' Elizabeth Wollaston declared in her no-nonsense fashion, and Kay gave up.

She sat silently in the car, her thoughts far from happy. She hadn't liked deceiving the other woman, and it sat heavily on her conscience. It was the quality of her silence that drew more than one look from Ben, though she wasn't aware of it. Finally, he spoke up.

'All right, what's troubling you?'

Kay started and glanced round. 'I should have told her she wasn't my aunt,' she explained heavily.

'She'll find out soon enough,' Ben answered grimly. 'As soon as the Press get a hold of the story, they'll have a field-day.'

Her heart sank as she thought of the media coverage he was referring to. 'Do they have to know?'

Ben gave a dry laugh. 'Hard to stop those ghouls finding out. There will have to be an investigation. The police will want to trace Ronnie Napier. Missing heiresses don't just turn up and fade into the scenery. You'll be news, like it or not.'

Kay shuddered, thinking of Jean Napier. 'They'll brand her a criminal, too, and she wasn't.'

He shot her a glance. 'The law might have other ideas. You'll have to be prepared for that.'

'Never! I'll never believe it, and neither would you if you'd known her!' she defended fiercely.

Ben's hands tightened on the wheel before he forced himself to relax. 'I'll take your word for it. All I'm saying is there's going to be a lot of mud-slinging. A lot of it will hurt, but I think you're strong enough to survive it.'

The certainty in his tone calmed her down. 'You do?'

Her surprise brought a wry smile to his lips. 'You fight me without any trouble,' he observed blandly.

A brief smile lightened her face momentarily. 'Fleet Street is minor league compared to you,' she admitted.

'See what I mean?' he laughed. 'A piece of cake!'

Kay laughed, then sighed, wondering how on earth she had ever thought she could resist him. When he was like this, she felt as if she could take on the world and win. Which, she thought wryly, was probably what she was going to have to do in the very near future. A prospect that occupied her thoughts for the remainder of the journey to Ben's house.

Ben carried the case inside and set it down in the hall, then strode into the lounge and poured himself a drink which he tossed off at one go. Turning to Kay, who had followed him and now hovered in the doorway frowning, he grimaced.

'Don't nag me. It's been a hell of a day, and I needed that. Can I get you one?' he offered, turning to replenish his own glass, sipping at it this time.

'Not for me.' She watched him, finding her eyes drawn to the tanned column of his throat, which flexed as he swallowed. He was altogether too potent an animal and far too tempting. It was crazy. With all the troubles she had, she could think only of how much she wanted him. How did he manage to divert her thoughts so easily? The answer was simple. Because nothing meant as much to her as he did, not even her pride. She needed him. If her life was to have a new beginning, perhaps it should start tonight, with him.

'If you continue to look at me like that, I won't be answerable,' Ben's voice came to her, soft and seductive, making her start.

Betraying colour washed into her cheeks. Had her thoughts been an open book to him? Did it really matter anyway? 'And just how am I looking?' she asked huskily, hugging her arms around her.

Ben eased his weight back against the sideboard, eyes gleaming. 'As if you'd like to ravish me on the spot.'

Heat enveloped her. 'Don't be ridiculous!'

One eyebrow shot up. 'You ought to be on the receiving end. You have very expressive eyes. A man could drown in them very easily.'

A man? 'But not you?'

He glanced at his watch. 'Not right now, anyway. I've got some calls to make. There's no way I will be returning to London for the next few days. Charles will have to stand in for me.'

At once her mind refocused. 'Are you going to tell him?'

'Not until we've seen Marsha,' he decided, setting his glass aside.

Kay clamped down hard on a wave of nervousness. 'Do you want to rush right over tonight?'

Ben shook his head. 'You've had just about enough for today. Tomorrow will do.' Pushing himself upright, he came over to her. 'Is there anyone you need to ring to explain you'll be away a few days?'

Already things were getting more complicated. 'My boss. I'll have to explain to him and ask for some leave,' she put forward, then felt a sharp pang of conscience. 'And Lance,' she offered, realising she hadn't thought about him for days.

Ben's expression was assured as he reached out to trace a finger over her lips. 'You'd better put him out of his misery, Kay.'

Confusingly, she was both thrilled and angered by the possessive tone. Why couldn't he be as unsure of her, as she was of him? 'Don't tell me what to do!' she warned, determined not to appear to be a pushover.

There was a flash of anger in those deep blue eyes. 'You know damn well you're not going to marry him now.'

In the mood she was in, it was the wrong tack to take. 'Do I really? Because you want an affair with me?'

His eyes narrowed. 'Because you don't respond to him the way you do to me!' he gritted out.

Her mind filled with incredulous wonder at the blatant double standard, and propelled her on. 'You intend to marry a woman you feel nothing for. I can't see the difference. You need an heir, I want security. Lance will give me that,' Kay argued, even though she knew it wasn't going to happen.

The angry set of his jaw was awesome. 'All the same, you won't marry him!' he declared forcefully.

The statement left her as breathlessly angry as him, while the root of his anger left her mystified. 'Why not?'

'Because I won't let you!'

Her lips parted in a soundless gasp. He wasn't just angry, he was almost beside himself, and all of a sudden she felt she was on the verge of something momentous. She swallowed. 'Why won't you let me marry him, Ben?' she asked softly. Her eyes searched his and witnessed an almost infinitesimal moment of shock before all expression was wiped out. She could almost see him take a step backwards though he didn't move.

When he spoke there was virtually no inflexion in his voice. It was as blank as his eyes. 'Why? Because you'd be making a terrible mistake. You're a member of the family now, and I couldn't let you do something you'd regret, not if speaking out could prevent it. I think of Peter and Connie as my brother and sister, and I'd do the same for them.'

The shock Kay experienced at his words rocked her to her very core, and left her pale, a cold lead weight in her stomach. 'Are you telling me that you and I are now virtually brother and sister?' she asked incredulously.

Ben shrugged, slipping his hands into his pockets and moving away. 'It will mean a bit of an adjustment, but you were right this afternoon, I couldn't seduce Kimberley the way I would Kay,' he returned smoothly.

This complete about-face stunned her. Only a moment ago he had been flirting with her, talking about drowning in her eyes! 'I don't believe you!' she cried with a ragged laugh.

He studied his toes. 'I could have guessed you wouldn't.'

Her mind whirled. 'What about us?'

He looked up again with a sigh. 'There is no us,' he replied bluntly.

At that her head went back. 'How dare you? You were the one who forced me to accept this attraction in the first place!'

Ben rubbed a hand around his neck, looking shame-faced. 'All I can say is, I didn't know then who you were.'

It was just too much to believe. By her sides her hands curled into fists, as if that could hold back the pain that threatened to overwhelm her. 'You're lying!' she charged. 'Why are you doing this?'

With a sympathetic look, he laid his hands on her shoulders. 'I'm not lying. I've suddenly seen how impossible our relationship is. Things change and we have to accept them as they are.'

She shrugged him off with an angry gesture, his touch almost a physical pain. 'I don't have to accept anything. *I* know only too well how things don't have to be the way they look!'

'By refusing to accept, you're only prolonging a distasteful situation,' Ben grated, then with a heavy sigh, he let his hands drop away. 'Listen, Kay, I didn't want to hurt you——' he began, only to halt as her fist slammed against his chest.

The very last thing he would ever know was just how much he had hurt her. 'You didn't hurt me. You couldn't. You've made me bloody angry! How dare you suggest you can just turn passion on and off like a light?' she cried, furiously angry and so deeply hurt that she felt as if she were breaking into a thousand pieces inside.

Ben set his jaw, although a nerve ticked away beside it. 'I happen to be older than you.'

Her eyes flashed tempestuously. 'Don't try to make out you're Methuselah, Ben Radford! I'm not that credulous!'

'No,' he admitted soberly, 'you're not. But the fact remains, things have changed. I'm sorry. Now, if you'll excuse me, I'll have to go or I'll miss Charles.'

Kay watched him walk out in impotent dismay. Emotions seethed inside her. An almost unbearable pain threatened to destroy her, and she summoned anger like a shield. She didn't for a moment believe this sudden change of heart, although she did believe he had changed his mind. She could have accepted that, but not the excuse he made. He was playing a game. A wicked, hurtful game. Because she knew he still wanted her. She might not be experienced, but she wasn't that naïve. Somehow she'd find out what it was and why, and then, so help her, she'd make him regret he ever dared toy with her!

Kay had dinner on a tray in her room. Not that she had felt much like eating. The earlier confrontation with Ben had taken most of her appetite away, and the telephone conversation she had had later with Lance had put paid to the rest. He hadn't been amused by her decision to stay away, nor by the fact that she wouldn't tell him why.

She hadn't intended, at that point, to tell him over the phone that it would be better if they didn't see each other again, feeling it was the sort of thing which should be done in person. However, his attitude roused her still simmering temper. She didn't like the way he talked to her as if she was already his wife and therefore the 'little woman'. She told him so, and the remainder of their brief conversation was heated and very much to the point. It ended with him very much on his dignity, informing her she wasn't the woman he had thought she was at all.

A fact she had to agree with herself. Not just because she now knew she wasn't Kay Napier, but because her response to Ben had revealed an unsuspected side of herself. It just wasn't possible for her to settle for second best. An acknowledgement that gave her no satisfaction, for, although she had reached the point where she had decided to enter into an affair with Ben and face the inevitable heartache later, he had declared himself out of the race.

It was recalling the manner in which he had chosen to do it which actually helped her eat the omelette and salad Bridie had prepared, because she chewed each mouthful with absent-minded anger. By the time she was finished, no nearer a solution to his despicable behaviour than she was at the start, she was surprised to look down and see an empty plate.

It was later, when she returned to the bedroom after showering and getting ready for bed, that her gaze fell on the case. Ben must have brought it up earlier, and it now stood on the floor by the dresser. Setting it on a chair, she opened it. She carefully lifted out the diary and the brown paper parcel, and carried both back to the bed. Curling up against the pillows, she rested the parcel on her knees and opened the diary at the beginning.

Life for Jean Napier had been made up of a series of highs and lows. It was clear she knew the type of man she had married, but she loved him so much that she constantly made excuses for him. The birth of Sarah had really been the highlight of her life. Reading between the lines, it was clear the marriage was always rocky; that was why the little girl had mattered so much. Both Jean and Ronnie loved her, which was a kind of saving grace in his favour.

Her death had been a devastating blow, but Jean's outpourings of guilt on to the pages showed her unstable state of mind. In her confusion she felt she was being punished for some unknown act, and that to have another child would somehow right the wrong. She was desperate to have another baby, and was inconsolable at her inability to conceive.

Then the next entries were all joyous. Ronnie said they'd adopt a little girl. He knew where to go. All Jean's worries were swept away. Her joy when 'K' was delivered was boundless, wiping out her uneasiness at having to move to Newcastle, leaving her family behind, and the proposed move south to London.

Kay read the final entry and closed the book. It had been like reading the life story of a stranger, but then that was precisely who Jean Napier was. She had never told Kay any of this. It had all happened in another life. It was doubtful if Jean ever suspected anything underhand, other than that the 'agency' the baby came from was dodgy. Ronnie had taken the money and run. And the tone of the two different diaries revealed that she hadn't really missed him. Had, in fact, found herself. She had been happier these last twenty-four years than she had ever been.

Kay remembered all those happy times of her growing years. She'd wanted for nothing that it was humanly possible to get. There had been plenty of love, she could never doubt that. Her mother had loved her and she had returned that love. She could never hate the woman who had raised her. Yet she felt strangely detached from it all now. Because it had been founded on a lie, and she felt cheated.

Putting the book aside, she folded back the brown paper and rested her hand on the soft, tiny garments, trying to feel that other life. A wave of deep sadness brought an ache to her chest and clogged her throat. A great sob broke from her, followed by another and another, and she thrust the covers aside, scrambling from the bed and rushing to the door.

Acting instinctively, she knew who she needed right then. Ben's room was along on the left, and she ran to it, thrusting it open so that it crashed back against a chair, bringing the man in the bed to instant wakefulness, sitting up to scrabble for the light and switch it on.

'What the hell . . . ?' Bare-chested, hand shielding his eyes from the glare, Ben stared at her.

Kay wasn't even aware that she was wringing her hands or of the tears tracing rivers down her cheeks. 'How could they do that to a little baby, Ben?' she demanded brokenly. 'How could they do that to *me*?'

Ben swore softly, and was out of the bed in a trice, covering his nakedness with a white terry robe. Then he was rounding the bed and drawing her into his arms, cradling her against his chest as if she were made of the finest china. He didn't try to stop her crying, merely absorbed the concussion of her body-shaking sobs and offered her the comfort she sought.

Only when sheer exhaustion quietened her and took the strength from her legs did he swing her up into his arms and carry her to his bed. Setting her down against the pillows, he would have left her then, to close the door, only her fingers had a death-grip on his robe. Sighing, he stretched out beside her and drew her once more into his warmth.

Kay, nerves worn to a frazzle, knew only a great sense of safety and relaxed, allowing the tears to dry. She felt empty, emotionally drained. Comforted by the warmth and strength of him, she sighed and uttered only one sad word, 'Why?'

Ben twisted his head to glance down at her. Tear-damp eyelashes rested fragilely against pale cheeks, and he swallowed hard. 'Because there are a lot of greedy people in the world, Kay, and a great many unhappy ones,' he answered in a whisper. 'Don't try to think about it. Just sleep. It will all be better in the morning.'

'Promise?' she challenged faintly.

Beside her, Ben grimaced, unseen. 'Oh, hell! Yes, I promise.'

From far away, she heard, and sighed. Vaguely she recalled there was a reason why she shouldn't be here, but it remained lost in a fog. 'It's OK, I won't hold you to it,' she murmured just before drifting away.

Ben's head fell back against the pillows. 'Didn't I say you were dangerous?' he said wryly, and closed his eyes.

CHAPTER EIGHT

IT WAS the chink of china that woke them at eight o'clock the next morning. Kay blinked, totally disorientated, fractionally alarmed that her pillow moved. Then she heard Bridie's voice, thick with disapproval.

'Will Miss Kay be requiring a cup, too?'

Ben's voice answered in barely concealed amusement. 'Yes, thank you, Bridie.'

There was a pause and another chink. 'I'll close the door on the way out, shall I?' Bridie added in a heavy tone as she finally left.

Kay's realisation of where she was came swiftly, and with it the memory of how they had parted yesterday. Now, in the cold light of day, her anger had hardened, temporarily cauterising a hurt that went deep. She wanted to wound him, too, despite his kindness to her last night. He couldn't treat her as he had and expect to get away with it. Her weapons might be few, but she'd use every one she had. Starting now. Steeling her face to reveal nothing of what she was feeling, she moved from her comfortable position, raising her head to look at Ben, finding his eyes were still fixed broodingly on the door.

'You've shocked her,' she said, and drew sleepy blue eyes her way in a lazy inspection. Her heart squeezed, anger fomenting. How could he look at her like that and still expect her to believe he no longer wanted her?

'Disappointed her,' he corrected. 'I have brought women here before. It's you that made the difference. She didn't expect to find you in my room.'

It was the cruellest irony to Kay to discover she could get to like waking up with him like this. Sleep had

141

softened him, and the overnight growth of beard on his chin made him rakishly attractive. It brought the taste of acid to her tongue. Yet when she spoke, her voice was sultry and husky. 'You should have explained that I turned up here in tears last night.'

He breathed in sharply, arrested. 'I could have,' he said slowly, 'but that would still have brought forth a lecture. Bridie has strict ideas on right and wrong.'

Kay dropped her eyes to hide the bitter curl of her lip, looking instead to where her hand rested on his robe, just over his heart. But Bridie didn't know that, according to Ben, she couldn't have found a safer place to sleep. Damn him for a liar! Well, Bridie had gone, the door was closed and Ben's guard was down. It was all she needed to challenge his statement of yesterday. She'd make him eat his words.

'I see.' Slowly her hand slipped beneath the robe and smoothed over the hot silky skin of his chest. 'She thinks I've been compromised. Does that mean you'll have to marry me now?' she taunted, and felt him tense instantly.

'There are laws about incestuous marriages,' he pointed out gruffly, and she looked up at once, hiding her anger beneath half-lowered lids, smiling like a cat, her voice a purr.

'But you're not my brother, are you, Ben? You're no relation at all,' and, to emphasise the point, she slowly ran her knee up his thigh.

Ben jerked away as if he'd been shot. 'Don't!' he ordered sharply.

Kay gave a husky laugh. 'Why? You know you don't really want me to.' Her brows lifted mockingly. 'Shall I prove it to you?' She lowered her head to the tanned skin of his throat, kissing him, tasting him with her tongue, determined to get a response, and getting it as she felt his pulse begin to race.

In the next instant he had taken a handful of her hair and tugged her head up. His eyes glittered. 'You damned little tease!' he growled, and just as swiftly rolled her on to her back, grinding his mouth down on hers.

It hurt, but there was pleasure in the pain for she could feel his body responding to hers. Her heart swelled with triumph as she returned every wild, heated caress of his hands and mouth. When his lips left hers to trail their way down to her breast, she arched against him, thrilling as he ground his hips against hers, letting her feel his need. Let him deny it now, if he could.

Yet before her lips could form the taunting question, Ben wrenched himself away from her, flinging himself from the bed with a hoarse denial. 'No!'

Eyes glittering like jewels, Kay came to her knees. 'No? Don't you mean yes?' she challenged, wanting her pound of flesh.

But Ben was recovering quickly, his eyes now the remote blue of outer space. 'Stop it, Kay. You're just making yourself cheap,' he declared in icy distaste.

The words took her breath away, freezing her blood and taking all the colour from her cheeks. An anger so intense that she felt she could scarcely contain it rose up inside her. 'Cheap!'

Fully composed once more, he raked his hands through his hair, tightened the belt of his robe and regarded her with hooded eyes, face set. 'What else would you call a woman who throws herself at a man?'

Painful colour came storming back, and she scrambled to her feet. 'Take that back!' she ordered thickly.

A nerve ticked in his jaw. 'If the truth hurts, you've only yourself to blame,' he informed her harshly. 'Now if you wouldn't mind leaving, I'd like to get dressed.'

To say anything more was beyond her right then. The words would have stuck in her throat. Sending him a withering look, she quickly left the room. Each furious step she took on the way back to her own bedroom was a dagger aimed at his heart. Once there she flung herself on to the bed, hands beating into the pillows, wishing it were him! How dared he call her cheap?

Rolling on to her back, she stared up at the ceiling. She'd pay him back for that. If it was the very last thing she did, she'd pay him back! Calling her cheap when he had been fully aroused himself! She'd show him, because he wasn't immune. Far from it. Tit for tat. He'd made her admit to wanting him and then he'd dropped her, and she'd make him admit it too. Then he could watch her walk away!

They left for the Endacotts' shortly after breakfast. Bridie had been all smiles as she prepared toast, so it was obvious to Kay that Ben had had a word with her. She clucked over the fact that neither Ben nor Kay ate very much, and once or twice Kay caught her smiling knowingly to herself.

Kay was grimly amused by the housekeeper's surmising. She had locked away hurt in a deep recess of her mind, feeding on anger. Plotting Ben's downfall was all she could allow herself to think of just now. When he appeared in the breakfast-room, she met his searching look with chin held high.

'We'll leave when you're ready,' he said abruptly. 'You might pack your case as well. Marsha will no doubt invite you to stay.'

Kay rose to her feet. 'It's already packed,' she informed him with cool politeness. She had telephoned an understanding employer, too, and arranged to take some of her holiday allowance.

'So eager to leave?' he drawled mockingly.

Her smile was lethal. 'I wouldn't want to be accused of being cheap and of outstaying my welcome, all in the same day. Besides, I've discovered an aversion to houses that reek of mendacity.'

Ben drew in his breath sharply. 'Don't push me too far, Kay.'

She threw her head back and laughed. 'Why, what will you do, hit me? But you're opposed to physical violence. Make love to me? Oh, but silly me. Of course you couldn't do that, because you don't want me. Do you?' she taunted back.

After a moment, when he seemed on the verge of a curt reply, Ben overcame the urge with a magnificent show of control. 'I'll fetch the car round. Meet me outside in ten minutes,' he ordered shortly, before going out again.

She was there in five, carrying the two small cases. Wordlessly, Ben stowed them in the back, before seeing her into her seat and taking his own. The journey, as was often the case, didn't seem to take so long the second time. Kay was surprised by her own calmness. In the space of a week her life had changed in more ways than one. She had found and lost love, and lost and found a mother. She didn't know yet what the latter would mean to her. All she could hope to do was meet her new family with an open mind.

Once again Marsha was on the top step to meet them. Whether she had been alerted by Ben or some other instinct, Kay didn't know, but she was aware of tension held firmly in check. Climbing from the car, she found her heart was beating faster as she stared up at the woman she now knew was her mother. It was impossible not to feel emotional when she thought of the years of faith and hope this woman had endured. Years that were now coming to an end.

Ben's hand on her arm made her start and glance round. Her first instinct was to pull away, but there was a gentleness in him as he scanned her face that made her hesitate. 'OK?'

She told herself not to read anything special into his manner. It was the occasion, not herself, which had produced it, and Marsha's presence. All the same, she did feel ridiculously warmed. Silently she nodded, and they moved forwards, mounting the steps to where Marsha waited, her smile coming and going, the only sign of stress. When they halted before her, her eyes went immediately to Ben.

'Well?' she urged tensely. 'Yes or no?'

The question surprised Kay, but, even as she was attempting to interpret its meaning, Ben was answering.

'Could it be anything but yes?'

Marsha uttered a broken cry, hands coming up to cover her lips as her eyes turned molten. Through them she feasted on Kay. 'Didn't I tell you? The second I saw her, I knew you'd brought my Kimberley back! I knew I couldn't be wrong!' she declared, reaching out one hand to him, which he gripped firmly.

Kay, who had still firmly believed Marsha didn't know who she was, digested this stunning revelation. Why hadn't she said something yesterday? she wondered, and almost immediately knew the answer. Because she hadn't dared to. After all this time, she hadn't dared to believe the evidence of her own eyes. But she had unburdened herself to Ben, and naturally his fondness for Marsha had made it easy for him to keep her suspicions secret. It seemed she was the only one who didn't know!

'Your instinct has never played you false, Marsha,' Ben was saying gruffly, patently moved.

Marsha laughed mistily, and turned to Kay. There was a moment when it seemed she didn't know quite what to do, then she raised her hands tentatively, ready to withdraw if she saw any sign that Kay should resent it. But when Kay remained still, gently she cupped her face. Even so Kay could feel their trembling and nearly broke up at the overwhelming love and joy on Marsha's face.

'My Kimberley,' she murmured, checking every feature as if to imprint it on her memory. Kay began to tremble, too, as, very tenderly, Marsha brushed a kiss on her forehead. 'Welcome home, darling. So very, very welcome home!' she greeted huskily, then with emotions warring on her mobile face, she bit her lip and stepped back, hands clasped tightly before her.

'Thank you, Ben, for bringing her.' Her glance swung to him then Kay, before she turned away with less than her usual grace.

Kay was in a state of utter turmoil. She had remained immobile because she had found it suddenly impossible to move. Marsha's emotion had hit her like a tidal wave, and the depth of her own response had stunned her. She hadn't expected to feel so strongly for someone she didn't know, nor to understand the reason for Marsha's discomfiture. Yet she did, and her actions were instinctive.

'Marsha.' The use of her name halted the other woman, and she turned. Even if Kay had been able to speak, she wouldn't have known what to say. Actions spoke louder. She held out her arms.

Marsha gasped, took a step towards her, then faltered. 'I...didn't think you'd want that. You don't know me.'

Kay had guessed that, and now painfully dredged up words. 'I think I'd like to know...what it's like to be...held by my real mother.'

There was no need to say more. Marsha swept her lost daughter into her arms and they both burst into tears. Yet it was a healing weeping that didn't last long before Marsha stepped back, wiping haphazardly at her eyes.

'Oh, dear, I promised myself I wouldn't do that, but I was so worried about how you would accept me. The last thing I wanted to be was cloying, and turn you right off. I haven't been able to eat a thing since yesterday, but now I could do with a good strong cup of tea,' she said with a happy smile.

'I think that's a good idea,' Kay agreed, glad that she hadn't held back. It hadn't felt strange at all, but right. As if, coming to the end of a long journey, here was peace.

'Come along in, then. My goodness, I don't know if I'm on my head or my heels, but do you know something? It feels so good, I don't care!' She laughed as if the years had been stripped away, then glanced over her shoulder at Ben, who hadn't moved. 'You're staying, aren't you, Ben?'

For one second, it seemed to Kay that he was about to refuse, but then he smiled. 'Of course. You go ahead. I've got to get something from the car, then I'll join you.'

Kay accompanied Marsha into what she called the family room, where a tea tray already sat on the coffee-table. She drew Kay down beside her on to a couch, looking quite serious for a moment.

'Before Ben comes, I think we ought to settle a couple of things, don't you? You're my daughter, but we're strangers, so it would be silly of me to expect you to call me Mother. Marsha will do very well. And I shall continue to call you Kay. After all, it is the pet form of names beginning with "K". Heavens, we might even have called you that ourselves. Anyway, I think that will make us all feel more comfortable, don't you agree?'

Kay produced a small smile. It had been bothering her, and she hadn't wanted to feel torn. 'I'd like that, for now at least. Perhaps one day...' She shrugged diffidently.

Marsha sighed and reached for the teapot. 'Plenty of time for that. We'll all have to feel our way, and we must resist trying to run before we can walk. I'm just so...overjoyed to have you here. There aren't words enough to tell you what it means to me.'

'But she'll have a good try,' Ben added as he entered and caught the last few words. 'Marsha loves to talk.' He placed the case down beside Kay's feet and took a chair by the fireplace.

Marsha handed over a cup of tea. 'If you must stir, do it to your tea.'

'Yes, Mother,' he agreed, tongue-in-cheek.

Marsha tutted, but said with satisfaction, 'He's a terrible tease. I don't know why we put up with him.'

'Because you're a sucker for stray lambs and lost causes,' he informed her over the top of his cup.

'Anything less lamb-like you're unlikely to find!' Kay retorted acidly.

Ben's teeth flashed whitely. 'You're hardly clawless yourself.'

Marsha stared from one to the other in astonishment. 'Goodness me, have you two quarrelled?'

Kay crossed her legs and stirred her tea before sending him a glance. 'Have we, Ben?'

'Call it a difference of opinion. Kay just refuses to back down.'

Her smile was brittle. 'That's because one of us is lying through his teeth.'

Marsha uttered a gurgling laugh, which had them both staring at her. 'I'm sorry, but it sounded just like old times, hearing the children squabbling.'

'And that puts us firmly in our place!' Ben declared wryly.

Kay wasn't quite so amused at being lumped in with the other members of the family, because that only bolstered his claim. Unable to argue the point, she set her cup down and reached for the case, removing the paper parcel. She held it out to Marsha who hastily disposed of her own cup to take it. Her gaze questioned them.

'We found these locked in that case at an aunt's house,' Kay began to explain, then faltered. 'That is, at the house of...' A gentle touch on her knees stopped her.

'At your aunt's house,' Marsha insisted gently. 'You don't have to try and protect me. I'm stronger than I look.'

Kay couldn't resist sending Ben a speaking look, for she had said the same thing. He acknowledged it with a dry smile, and she went on. 'Anyway, we wondered if you'd recognise them.'

Marsha must have had some instinct as to what it contained, because for a moment she did nothing more than look at the wrapping. Eventually, though, she parted the paper and fingered the contents.

'Yes, I recognise them,' she admitted sadly. 'You were wearing them the day you disappeared. I remember thinking that you'd soon outgrow them. You were growing so fast, your father said we'd created a giant.' With a sigh she shook her head, surreptitiously wiping away moisture from her eyes, then rose and went to a bookcase and brought back a framed photograph. 'This was taken not long before you disappeared. You're wearing the same clothes.'

Kay took it, recognising the clothes at once, but also, to her surprise, seeing something of herself in the baby's rounded features. There had never been any photographs like these at home, only the old ones she had found after her 'mother' died. Which brought her to something she knew she had to say.

'The people who took me...we don't know if there was more than one person involved, but... One of them was the husband of the woman I always thought was my mother.'

Marsha was clearly shocked, and turned to Ben for confirmation. He nodded. 'It's true.'

'But she knew nothing about it,' Kay insisted, hastily. 'I have her diaries. You only have to read them to know that. She lost her own child and wanted another one. Ronnie told her I came from a backstreet agency, and she didn't think to question it. Besides, he left her the minute they reached London. He was guilty but she wasn't.' She looked Marsha squarely in the eye. 'You have to know that I could never hate her just because her husband stole me from you. She loved me, and I always loved her. I'm sorry.'

There was silence in the room for a space of a heartbeat, then Marsha sighed. 'There's no need to apologise. I am glad you told me, though, because I think we have to be honest with each other. I accept your opinion, which has to be good, because you appear to have convinced Ben—no mean thing, I can tell you. For myself, I know I could never forgive the people who took you away. I am also quite unbearably jealous of the woman who raised you, and jealous of the years that should have been mine. I can only say she did a good job of raising you, and perhaps I'll accept that better when I know about her. Some day soon, we must talk about her, but not today. Today is for us, yes?'

Kay was relieved. It wouldn't be easy for either of them, and there would be worse days to come, but with goodwill they would find their way through to understanding. So she smiled. 'Yes.'

'Then come over here and meet the rest of your family,' Marsha invited, drawing her over to the bookcase. 'You have a brother and sister, you know. Peter's in America, so I'm afraid you won't meet him just yet, but there's Connie, and of course Charles, your grandfather.'

'We've met, although I didn't know who he was at the time,' Kay admitted, finding herself intrigued by her new family when she had thought she was alone in the world.

'Once seen, never forgotten! He'll be delighted. We'll have to have a party to introduce you to everyone, because you have aunts, uncles and cousins, too,' Marsha declared with a laugh, before reaching for another photograph which she handled lovingly. 'But first, I want to introduce you to your father.'

As Kay took the photograph of the man who had sired her, and whom she would now never know, Ben stood up. 'I'm going to leave you two alone for a while. If you've no objection, I'll use the study. I must ring

Charles and the police. I thought I'd give Nita a ring,
too. She probably thinks I've deserted her.'

Kay knew that last message was meant for her, and
her lips compressed tightly. Marsha, however, saw
nothing amiss and smiled at him. 'Of course, dear. Do
I know this Nita?'

'You haven't met her, but perhaps I'll introduce you
one day soon,' Ben answered easily.

Kay's fingers tightened on the picture. 'Why don't you
invite her up for the party?'

His look was intended to slay her on the spot. 'Now
why didn't I think of that?'

She sent him a pitying look. 'Because that's the sort
of thing sisters are here to do. I've got to get into the
swing of it, because that is how you see me, isn't it, as
a sister?' It did her good to see the way his chest rose
and fell agitatedly.

Yet his expression was bland. 'Precisely. Now you're
getting it, try not to forget again.' The warning was
implicit.

'Remind me to tie a knot in my hankie,' she cooed
back sweetly as he left them.

Marsha sighed heavily. 'You two are behaving most
mysteriously, but I won't pry. No doubt you'll explain
in your own good time.' She sounded light-hearted, but
she was, in fact, extremely thoughtful.

'You were going to tell me about my father,' Kay reminded her gently, although her eyes couldn't help
drifting to the door Ben had disappeared through. A
wave of jealousy caught her as she imagined him talking
to Nita, and she was unaware of how the pain was mirrored on her face.

Marsha saw, and wondered.

Ben stayed for lunch, spending most of the time be-
forehand on the telephone in the study. Although Kay
was dying to know what he had said to Nita, she'd cut

her tongue out before she asked. Charles, he informed them, had had to be restrained from dropping everything and rushing north. He had finally been persuaded to leave it until Wednesday when he could bring Connie back with him.

The police had been a different matter. There was nobody on the current force who had worked on the case, which had meant a great deal of explaining had had to be done. They were, naturally, interested at the turn of events, and highly sceptical. Ben had arranged for a senior detective to come and interview Kay the next day.

The subject lasted the entire meal, and immediately afterwards Ben made his excuses. Although Marsha pressed him to stay, he was adamant, and she wasn't able to argue against his statement that she and Kay needed to be alone to get to know each other. Resigning gracefully, she linked arms with her daughter and they walked with him out to his car.

'Drive carefully, Ben,' Marsha cautioned, and he gave her a broad smile.

'Don't I always? Now, don't you two stay up chatting all night. You don't have to do all your catching up at one go,' he teased her, bending to give her a hug and a kiss.

'Don't I get a sisterly kiss, too?' Kay couldn't resist saying, when he appeared about to leave without sparing her a glance. She might have to put up with his pretence, but she'd be damned if she'd be ignored.

Ben's hesitation was so small that it could have been overlooked. Then he smiled. 'Of course,' and, holding her by the shoulders, bent to brush her cheek.

Only Kay was having none of that. With a split-second to spare she swiftly turned her head, and the kiss that should have landed on her cheek found her mouth. She felt him go rigid and pressed home her advantage, teasing his lips with her tongue. Ben caught his breath and she

felt him tense to pull away, then gasped as his tongue
thrust into her mouth, ravaging her senses for all too
brief a time, before he pulled free and turned away.

Dragging in air, she experienced a moment of triumph
at her small victory. However, the smile faded as he drove
off, and she stared after the car with a heavy heart. Now
that he was gone, she felt deathly tired.

'Kay?' Marsha's voice interrupted her gloomy
thoughts, and she half turned. 'You look as if you've
lost a pound and found a penny. Can it be that bad?'
she questioned gently.

Kay couldn't stop her eyes from straying to the now
empty drive. 'I'm just feeling maudlin. It will pass.' She
fervently hoped so.

'Are you very much in love with him?'

Her heart lurched painfully, and Kay turned wild, disbelieving eyes on Marsha. Somehow she forced a laugh.
'In love? With Ben? Don't be silly! I scarcely know him.
Besides...' Her attempted humour deserted her. 'There
wouldn't be any point.'

Marsha came closer and slipped her arm through
Kay's. 'Let's walk, shall we? The gardens here are very
soothing,' she said as she steered them down the steps
and round the corner of the house. 'Edward and I designed the gardens soon after we were married, but it's
been a lifetime's work. I fell in love with him on sight,
though it took me a while to realise it.'

Kay wasn't really in the mood to hear these sort of
reminiscences, especially if they were designed to make
her feel better. 'Marsha, I know you mean well, but...'

Her mother laughed. 'You're going to tell me to mind
my own business. You're very right, naturally, but please,
hear me out. You see, I happen to think the best thing
that could happen to Ben would be to fall in love. He's
isolated himself too long. Although I understand why,
I can only abhor it. Let's sit here.' They had come to a
small gazebo with a stone bench inside.

Kay sat obediently, her eyes tracing the tranquil beauty of the gardens. 'I don't know why you're telling me all this. You know Ben doesn't believe in love. In fact, he never enters into an affair without making that point very clear!' she said bitterly.

Marsha's brows rose. 'I see. Are you having an affair with him?'

Kay squirmed in her seat, wishing she hadn't revealed so much. But it seemed ridiculous not to go on. 'I thought I was, until yesterday.'

'I think you'll have to explain that remark,' Marsha said, in some amusement, and Kay sighed.

'Ben and I are...were attracted to each other. He wánted an affair, and...'

'Because you love him, you agreed?'

Kay studied her mother helplessly, and nodded. 'I decided I'd rather have him for a while than not at all. I accepted that he couldn't love me. I was prepared to take the risk.'

Marsha took one of Kay's hands in hers. 'Darling, it isn't that Ben can't love anyone, it's that he won't. I think you should understand why. Ben was part of a very close family. They did everything together—his mother, father and younger brother. They used to holiday together, too, even though it wasn't fashionable for a teenager. To cut a long story short, when Ben was eighteen, instead of going with the family, he had to remain here to take some important exams. His parents and brother went to the South of France.' Fractionally she paused in her tale. 'It was the year of the most dreadful forest fires. The three of them were caught in one. Ben was devastated. It was awful to see him withdraw into himself. From that day he refused to love anyone, because he couldn't bear to lose them the way he lost his family.'

'How awful,' Kay murmured, her heart aching for the youth who had had to face such a dreadful tragedy.

'Awful indeed. I can't bear to see him live so super-
ficially when I know he's capable of loving very deeply.
But if I take him to task, he just laughs and says he's
perfectly happy.'

'But he seems to love you, and your family,' Kay con-
tested, frowning.

'Yes, I believe he does, although he chooses to call it
looking after the family interests. We're a foster family,
I suppose you'd call it. Only so close. He can be involved without being involved. I don't suppose he even
realises he's fooling himself.' Marsha's sigh was sad and
angry. 'It's wrong for him to live this way. He needs
someone to love, and someone to love him. Kay, you'd
be so perfect for him.'

Kay blinked away tears, chin jutting pugnaciously. 'I
think so too, but he doesn't want perfection.'

Marsha bit her lip. 'What does he want?'

Kay saw red just at the thought. 'He wants a sister,'
she said fiercely.

'Ben said that?' Marsha interrupted faintly.

Kay nodded. 'He had the gall to tell me he wouldn't
let me marry Lance.' Anger welled anew at the memory.
'He said, now that I was part of the family, he couldn't
let me make such a bad mistake,' she went on furiously.

Marsha blinked. 'And you believed him?'

'No, I did not!' Kay snapped, touched on the raw. 'I
may have been stupid enough to fall in love with him,
but I'm intelligent enough to know a lie when I hear it!'

'So what are you going to do?'

'Make him sorry! Make him eat his words! Make
him . . .'

Marsha swallowed a bubble of laughter. 'Love you?'
she suggested gently.

Kay winced. 'No, he won't do that.'

'Do you know, Kay, I've known Ben a long time, and
it's my belief he does love you? At the moment he's
fighting it the only way he knows how. Poor Ben, he

thinks sisters are nice safe people to have around. I wonder how long it will take him to realise the frying-pan was infinitely more comfortable than the fire?'

Kay sat up straighter. She'd only thought of revenge, but what if Marsha was right? If loving meant wanting to her, then it might be the same for Ben. If so, then the reward would be even greater. 'It would take a miracle,' Kay murmured, half to herself.

'But who knows better than us that miracles do happen?' Marsha concluded, and there was nothing Kay could say to that.

CHAPTER NINE

IN THE days immediately following, Kay had very little opportunity to put her plan into action. To begin with the police came and conducted a lengthy interview, before taking away all the evidence that pointed to her being Kimberley Endacott. Then, as Ben had predicted, the news broke nationally and they were inundated with newspaper and media people.

Ben proved to be a tower of strength. During the worst of the madness, he virtually haunted the house. He was never very far away, and whenever Kay needed him he was there. But while she was grateful for his presence, for keeping the hordes at bay, all her attempts at private conversation were thwarted. Gradually it dawned on her that he was responsible, because, although he was with her, he was always friendly and polite, but emotionally remote. It was as if he had never responded to her as wildly as she had him. It stung, and made her more determined to break through the wall he had erected between them.

The opportunity came about by pure chance. Walking out to join her mother on the lawn, she discovered Ben had arrived. Neither had heard her silent approach, and she eavesdropped shamelessly.

'My goodness, we do seem to be seeing a lot of you these days, Ben,' Marsha was saying, with a teasing smile. 'I wonder what the attraction is?'

'You know I couldn't let you cope on your own,' Ben explained, from his relaxed position on the soft grass at her side.

158

Marsha sighed. 'And there was I getting all romantic, thinking it was due to my lovely daughter.'

Ben laughed easily. 'As she's the cause of all the brouhaha, you're right.'

'Don't you like her, Ben?'

He reached across to briefly clasp her hand. 'I like all your children, Marsha. Kay's lovely, but that's it as far as I'm concerned.'

Kay winced at the pain of his careless tone, and decided she'd heard enough. 'He's just being brotherly,' she declared, not without a trace of sarcasm, making them both jump. 'Which reminds me, I haven't had the chance to thank you properly for all your help,' she added, and, dropping to her knees beside him, leant across to kiss him.

This time it was Ben who moved swiftly to avert his face, and her lips found his cheek. 'Coward!' she jeered, for his ears alone, and felt him tense.

Strong hands came up to clasp her shoulders. 'Someone ought to spank you!' he grated, and Kay laughed grimly.

'Do you mean you? Is it wise? Once you've got your hands on me, you might not want to let go!' she goaded in a whisper.

'Behave yourself!' Ben gritted through his teeth, and pushed her away so that she sat down abruptly.

Marsha rose with a laugh. 'Oh, dear, I have this motherly urge to smack you both. I've just remembered I have a phone call to make. Try not to have murdered each other by the time I get back!' she advised as she walked off.

Ben waited until she was out of earshot before sending Kay a withering look. 'What the hell are you trying to do?'

'Seduce you?' she offered lightly, but not without a lurch of her heart.

He swore. 'God, don't you have any pride at all?' he charged, getting up and running a hand round his neck.

Kay flushed but lifted her chin. 'As a matter of fact, I do. That's why I refuse to accept your lies. Peter's my brother, not you. You never could be, and you don't want to be. Admit it.'

Angrily he came over to her and jerked her to her feet. 'When are you going to get it through your head that there will never be anything between us?' he demanded roughly.

She placed her hand over his heart. 'When your body stops responding to mine. When your heart doesn't race when you're close to me,' she declared, and raised her eyes to his. 'It's racing now, just like mine, Ben.'

Blue eyes flashed warning signals as he brushed her hand aside. 'You're damn right it is. But don't mistake it for anything save anger. I can take just so much, but there's a limit to my patience. Keep up these games and you'll find out what happens when it does run out. So if you're very wise, you'll stay out of my way from now on.'

Kay crossed her arms to hide the way her hands trembled. 'No, I won't, not until you're honest with me.'

Ben's face could have been carved from stone. 'So that's the way you want it. OK, but don't expect me to pull my punches. Do your worst, Kay, but you'll give in before I do.'

Her heart quailed for a moment, but then her fighting spirit rose. 'Don't bet on it. You're a fraud, Ben Radford, and I'm going to prove it.'

'You can try, but there's nothing to prove. I don't want you, Kay. I don't want to hurt you, but I will if I have to,' he warned grimly, and turned his back on her and walked away.

Kay stared after him, wondering just what she'd let herself in for. It was a risk, because he had the power to hurt her even more deeply than he had. But it was a risk worth taking, because someone who didn't care wouldn't fight as strongly as Ben was. That alone gave her hope.

On Wednesday evening her sister Connie and Sir Charles were due to arrive, having driven up from London. Kay was nervous. Apart from Marsha, she had yet to meet other members of her immediate family. She needn't have worried. Neither showed any doubt as to who she was, and Sir Charles was too overcome to say a word, subjecting her instead to a bone-crushing hug before retreating to the fireplace and concentrating fixedly on filling his ubiquitous pipe.

More than a little misty-eyed herself, Kay was left to face her new sister, who was in the process of subjecting her to a minute study. Connie was the image of her mother, save for her dark brown hair and eyes. Her charming face creased into a smile as she witnessed Kay's nervousness.

'When Ben told me, I couldn't believe it, but I can see he was right. There's a look of Grandmother Endacott about you—in the eyes. And that hair! What wouldn't I give to have it! You *must* let me paint you. You and Mother together,' Connie exclaimed effusively.

Never having had a sister, Kay hadn't known what to expect. 'You don't resent me, then?' It was her greatest fear.

With the impulsiveness of her nature, Connie gave Kay a hug. 'Don't be silly. My little sister? I cried for weeks when you disappeared.' There was a suspicion of moisture in her eyes when she stepped back, shaking her head. 'I still can't believe it, but I'm so happy. We all are. It's a dream come true,' she exclaimed, then a movement across the room drew her eye and she squealed. 'Ben!'

Kay's nerves quivered, as they had an increasing tendency to do at the mere mention of his name, and she turned as he came into the room. In a black dinner suit that fit him to perfection, he quite took her breath away. He looked devastatingly handsome, and totally at ease, his face relaxed into a broad grin.

'I might have known you were the maniac who nearly drove me off the road,' he declared as he received her into his arms, ignoring her fist thumping into his shoulder. 'How's my favourite artist?'

Over Connie's shoulder their eyes met, and Kay breathed in sharply at the remoteness there. His lips curved in satisfaction, and he came across to brush a kiss on her cheek.

'And how's the newest member of the family?'

So that was how he intended to play it? Well, she wasn't about to join in. 'All the better for seeing you!' she answered brightly.

There was a momentary flash of annoyance in his eyes before he masked it. 'You're nothing but a flirt. Connie, you'll have to take your little sister in hand,' he advised her with a grin.

Kay raised her eyebrows. 'Why bring Connie into it? You'd have much more fun doing it yourself.'

'I've got much better things to do with my time than waste it on spoilt little cats who don't know when to sheath their claws,' he returned smoothly.

Anger flared in her eyes. 'But Ben, that wasn't what you were saying a few days ago!' she protested with a pout.

To her chagrin, he merely laughed. 'That's because I was filling in time. I don't normally play out of my league.'

That cut, as it was meant to do, and her response was instinctive. 'Oh, and I suppose Nita's in the major league, is she?'

'Nita's in a class of her own; you'll never match her. Now, if you'll excuse me, I'd better go and say hello to Marsha and Sir Charles.'

'Well!' exclaimed Connie, from beside her, as they both turned to watch him. 'That was interesting. Don't tell me you two have argued?' she asked incredulously.

Kay dragged her angry eyes away from the attractive figure he cut. 'Ben and I have a difference of opinion, and neither of us is prepared to give in.'

Connie gave Kay a searching look, then glanced over at Ben. 'He's gorgeous, isn't he?' she murmured slyly. 'All that sex appeal in just one man! It's not fair on us women. I've often thought of making a play for him myself.' Her laugh was light and infectious.

Kay couldn't laugh. 'Don't even think of it. You'd be wasting your time,' she warned far more curtly than she'd intended. Fearing she might have revealed too much, she forced a smile to her lips. 'You're family, Connie, so he just wouldn't play.'

Her sister looked puzzled. 'No, I know,' she agreed in an odd voice, before tactfully changing the subject. 'Anyway, before I forget, I've got your case outside. I hope I chose the right things.'

It was one of the many things Ben had arranged, that Connie should bring up fresh clothes from Kay's flat. 'I'm sure you have,' she smiled reassuringly.

'Listen, seeing how we seem to be ignored, why don't we go up to your room and unpack?' Connie suggested, taking Kay's arm. 'We can chat, while I watch! You don't know how much I've missed having a sister I can gossip with!'

Laughing, Kay allowed herself to be led away. Yet she couldn't resist one last look back, and her nerves leapt as she found Ben watching her. In her room, Connie was as good as her word. She kept up a humorous monologue, revealing an unsuspected ability to mimic, which raised Kay's spirits considerably. The case had been crammed full, much to Kay's amusement, but at least she now had a wider choice of clothes.

'Don't mind me talking so much.' Connie took a break from her one-sided conversation. 'I always do when I'm nervous.'

'You were nervous?' Kay gave a disbelieving laugh.

Connie shrugged. 'I was afraid I might not like you, or you me, when I've so longed for this.'

Kay sank down on the dressing-table stool and thoughtfully picked up her hairbrush. 'I never looked at it that way,' she admitted, realising once again that this was not an easy situation for any of them. 'All I was afraid of was that you'd think I was a fortune-hunter.'

Connie's animated face became serious. 'We've had our share of those, and I wouldn't be honest if I said it hadn't occurred to me, but when Ben explained how it all came about I knew that couldn't be true,' her sister admitted honestly.

Kay shuddered. 'I wish the Press were as easy to convince as you. They've been having a field-day.' Lurid headlines had been splashed over the covers of the dailies.

'Tell me about it! They make me so angry with their stories. The sooner the police finish their investigation, the better. Perhaps then we can all start to live normal lives again.'

Kay wished that too, although precisely what normal would be for her she wasn't quite sure yet. 'We'd better go down,' she advised as she finished brushing her hair. 'Marsha will be wondering what we're up to.' She caught Connie's frown and her smile faded. 'What is it?'

Connie bit her lip. 'I guess I'm not used to you calling Mother Marsha. It makes me see just how difficult it must be for you. How do you cope? I mean, it must all be so strange!'

That was an understatement, Kay mused wryly as she opened the door. 'It is, but you're all making it so easy for me to fit in.'

Her sister led the way out. 'You sound like Mother. I bet you've got her stoical spirit too. I'm far too temperamental. I'd be climbing walls!' she mocked herself. 'I expect that's part and parcel of what I do. I dabble in oils, you know,' she went on grandiosely, spoiling the effect with a gurgling laugh.

Kay responded with a laugh, realising there was no side to her sister. 'I gathered. Tell me about it. I'm afraid I'm rather ignorant about art.'

Never averse to talking about her favourite subject, Connie obliged until dinner was announced. Kay found herself seated next to Ben, which she knew didn't please him by the rigid set of his jaw. Conversation sparkled and she found herself laughing and joining in easily. However, she was fully aware that Ben rarely aimed a remark directly to her. When a lull fell while coffee was served, she was quick to mention it.

'Ignoring me won't make me go away, you know,' she informed him caustically.

He looked at her coldly. 'Nothing seems to. I've never known a woman with so little self-respect.'

He meant to hurt her and he succeeded, but she was quick to retaliate. Letting her napkin slip to the floor, on the pretext of picking it up again, she allowed her hand to settle on the top of his thigh, and was rewarded to feel him flinch. Lingering a shade longer, she sat up and tipped him an enquiring glance.

'Is something wrong?'

Like a vice, his hand fastened on her wrist, making her gasp and bite her lip. 'Do that again and, regardless of the audience, you'll get the thrashing you deserve!' he warned in a harsh whisper.

Her eyes flashed storm warnings. 'Promises, promises. You wouldn't dare touch me, and you know it. You could just as easily end up kissing me!'

Ben's smile was purely for anyone watching. 'Do you want to try it and see?'

Her stomach knotted but she refused to back down. 'Do you?'

They were locked in a kind of stalemate when Connie's voice broke in. 'Hey, you two, is this a private conversation or can anyone join in?'

Her teasing tone startled them both, and Ben released Kay so sharply that her arm flew up and collided with the coffee-cup Connie was just about to set down. The contents fell right into Ben's lap, and he shot to his feet with a muffled oath.

Before Kay could apologise for the accident, he turned and strode from the room. After a moment's indecision, Kay excused herself and followed. She found him in the downstairs cloakroom. He looked up swiftly as she entered, and scowled.

'Can I help?' she offered huskily, watching as he dabbed away with a handkerchief.

A harsh laugh left his throat. 'I think you've done enough, don't you?'

She flinched at his tone, but persevered. 'It was an accident.'

Blue eyes swept over her coldly. 'Like the napkin, hmn?'

Kay advanced a few paces. 'That was different. Look, if the coffee was hot, you may have burnt yourself. Why don't you take your trousers off?' she suggested helpfully.

'I'm not burned, so you can save your concern. You can also leave and let me get on with cleaning myself up,' he ordered icily.

Reluctant to go, Kay watched his ineffectual dabbing. 'You're just making it worse. Here, let me do it, please.'

For a moment Ben simply stared at her, then a strange look came into his eyes and he held out the cloth. 'All right, if it will please you,' he agreed silkily, and sat down on the toilet, legs slightly apart.

Suddenly, it seemed to Kay as if there was very little air left in the room, and her heart began to race. Strangely uncertain, she took the cloth and moistened it under the tap before dropping to her knees and starting to rub at the stains on his legs. The intimacy of the action struck her at once. Above her head she could hear Ben breathing steadily, could feel the brush of air passing over her nape. She bit her lip, concentrating on the job in hand, but found instead that she was intensely aware of his strong thighs outlined by the soft material. She faltered to a stop and raised wide, stormy eyes to his.

Ben's gaze was as cold and angry as the North Atlantic. 'Enjoying yourself? Now what am I supposed to do, take you in a rage of anger and disgust? Is that what you want to drive me to? Is that what it would take to stop you?'

Appalled, she stared at him. 'No!' The denial was forced from a tight throat. 'I don't...I didn't... But it wouldn't be like that, would it?'

For an aeon he just looked at her, a war waging in his eyes, a nerve ticking away in his jaw. 'Get out of here, Kay.'

'No, I can't. I won't go until you admit you couldn't take me in anger because you love me.'

All colour seemed to leave him. When he spoke, it was in a voice so desolate it brought smarting tears to her eyes. 'I'm sorry. I don't love you, Kay, I never did. Even if it was possible for me to love someone, then that someone would never be you.' His eyes fell to hers. 'Now will you go?'

A crippling pain made it impossible for her to move, so it was Ben who rose. Yet the worst of it was, he did so with such gentleness that it quite broke her heart.

At the door he paused. 'I was going to tell you, I have to go back to London tomorrow, but I'll be back for the party on Sunday.' When she didn't reply, he added, 'Will you be all right?'

She looked at him then, her eyes searching his, but the shutters came down and she grimaced. 'If I say no, will you end this silly game?' she asked and watched him close up. 'I didn't think so. Goodbye, Ben,' she sighed, and didn't allow the tears to fall until he had gone.

On Friday the police returned to tell them that their enquiries so far did indeed confirm that Kay was the missing Kimberley Endacott.

'What a relief,' Marsha declared, after they had gone. 'Not that I doubted, but it's good to have it confirmed.'

'And now we can go ahead with the party for Kay,' Connie went on enthusiastically. She had awarded herself a holiday to get to know her sister.

Kay, who could quite well have done without the party, had no intention of saying so, for two reasons. One, she wouldn't dream of hurting her family's feelings. Two... well, two concerned Ben. She had done a great deal of thinking after the tears had stopped. He had said he had stopped wanting her when he found out who she was, but she recalled that day down by the waterfall. He had still wanted her then, but he had also had reason to believe she was Kimberley. So that couldn't have been the reason for his sudden about-face. He had denied loving her, but in such a way that, in retrospect, it seemed to her that it had hurt him to say it.

While it had hurt her, so did the knowledge that in all their recent confrontations she had never told him she loved him. The realisation came too late. He had already gone, leaving only the promise of returning for the party that weekend. And that was where she planned to gamble everything on one bold throw. To tell the truth and shame the devil. If that didn't work... the future didn't bear contemplating.

So on Sunday evening, Kay went upstairs early to make her preparations. She took a long, leisurely bath in water scented with her favourite perfume, before donning sinfully expensive underwear and doing her make-up. As she stepped into the dress she had dragged Connie into Newcastle to help her buy, she couldn't help feeling both nervous and excited. Femininely, she wanted him to see her in it. She knew it made her look good. The blue was a perfect foil for her hair, and the silky fabric clung to every curve lovingly. Connie had fingered the tiny straps and declared it would knock their eyes out, but Kay was thinking of only one man. What she hoped to achieve was the triumph of faith over years of self-imposed emotional isolation. She was going for broke because she knew she had nothing to lose.

However, when Ben still hadn't shown up after the flood of arrivals began to slow to a trickle, a sick despair churned in her stomach. She was stationed in the hall with Marsha and Sir Charles to receive the guests, but her antennae had been attuned to only one arrival. With each passing minute she grew more and more certain he wasn't going to come. Then, just as they were about to go and join the party, Kay felt a positive charge zing in the air, and swung back to the door. He had come after all.

Her eyes were at once riveted to his magnetic presence in black dinner suit and brilliant white shirt. Relief warred with an intense pleasure, so that she was unaware, for a vital moment or two, that he was not alone. When that fact registered, she stared at the slim brunette on his arm in blank bewilderment. Since Kay was rendered speechless, it was left to Marsha to break the suddenly brittle silence.

'You're late, Ben. We'd almost given you up,' she declared, her arm slipping bracingly about Kay's waist.

Crossing the floor, he kissed Marsha's cheeks and shook Charles by the hand. 'My fault, I'm afraid. The phone rang at the last minute.'

'Trouble, Ben?' Sir Charles enquired instantly.

'Nothing to worry about.' Finally he turned to Kay's frozen figure. 'Kay, how are you?'

Kay regained her composure. 'I'm well, thank you. Won't you introduce us?' she invited, giving the sultry beauty, in her clinging red sheath, a faint smile. Not that she thought it was really necessary. She could make a good guess at the woman's identity.

'Kay, this is Nita Moore,' Ben obliged. 'Nita, say hello to the newly restored Kay Endacott, her mother and grandfather.'

Nita flashed them a friendly smile as she shook hands. 'I'm pleased to meet you all. I told Ben he shouldn't inflict a stranger on you at such a time, but he insisted.'

'I knew you wouldn't mind,' Ben smiled at Marsha, who suddenly smiled back broadly.

'Not at all, Ben. Miss Moore is quite welcome. I don't even know why I was surprised for a moment. It's just the sort of thing you would do. We understand, don't we, Kay?'

Kay understood only too well, and suddenly she felt like laughing. Oh, Ben! Who was using someone like a talisman now? 'Of course. Actually, I feel I know you, Nita. Ben's spoken of you often,' she said brightly. 'Grandfather, would you take Nita and get her a drink? I'd like to talk to Ben for a moment.'

Nothing loath, Sir Charles held out his arm, preening. 'My pleasure. You must tell me what it is you do,' they heard him say as he led her away.

Marsha took one look at Ben's closed expression and gave Kay's arm a squeeze. 'I'll go and circulate. Don't stay out here too long, you two,' she cautioned.

Ben barely waited until she was out of sight before letting off his opening salvo. 'What game are you playing?'

Kay, knowing it was make or break, took the bull by the horns. 'The same one as you, I thought,' she quipped.

He wasn't amused by her levity. 'That's no answer! Why did you get rid of Nita?'

She raised one smooth eyebrow. 'Why did you bring her?'

He ground his teeth, eyes narrowing. 'Stop trying to be clever and tell me the truth.'

Having rapidly reached the point of no return, Kay paled a little but wasn't about to falter now. 'Very well. You want to know the truth? Well the truth is I couldn't tell you I loved you with your bodyguard present, could I?' she said, knowing she'd never done anything as brave as this—laying her heart at his feet.

Whatever Ben had been expecting, it couldn't have been that for his head went back as if she'd struck him, and all his colour drained away. 'What?'

Her heart knocked. 'You heard me. Now it's your turn to tell *me* the truth. Do you love me, Ben?' she challenged softly, eyes unconsciously beseeching.

There was a moment or two when she thought she had won, but then he took a step away from her, a nerve ticking in his jaw. 'Nita and I are going to be married,' he declared thickly.

Kay swallowed hard on a wave of nausea. Feeling punch-drunk, somehow she managed to form words. 'Doesn't what I said mean anything to you?'

He stiffened. 'Naturally I'm honoured, but it changes nothing.'

A strained laugh tumbled from her lips. 'Honoured!' Hastily she dragged in air. 'You mean to go through with it?'

'Surely you know by now that I don't say what I don't mean.'

'Spoken like the true Ben Radford we all know and . . . love.' Her voice broke, and it was a second or two before she could go on. 'I've made rather a fool of myself, haven't I? It seems I'm always embarrassing you. But that hardly matters any more, does it? You've made certain it won't happen again. It only remains for me to wish you both happy.' Reaching the end of her tether, she pressed a hand to a throbbing temple and made a caricature of a smile. 'You'll excuse me now, I have to circulate.'

Plunging into the crowded lounge, she avoided people by instinct, her sight being nothing but a blur. She only stopped her headlong flight when firm yet gentle hands caught her arm.

'Kay?' Marsha's voice was thick with concern. 'Whatever's the matter? Ben?'

Kay stiffened, blinking back the tears, unaware that he had followed her.

'I said...something that upset her, Marsha. I'm sorry,' Ben's taut voice explained from behind her.

'You mustn't apologise!' Kay exclaimed, swinging round. 'It had to be said.' Her eyes challenged his. 'You must wish him happy, Marsha. He and Nita are to be married!'

'Is this true?' Marsha demanded.

Ben held Kay's eyes. 'Yes,' he confirmed, and she turned her back on him.

'Then you'd better go and join her, hadn't you?' Marsha suggested pointedly, and, after a wordless exchange, he strode away stiff-backed.

The minute he was gone, Kay looked round. 'It's my own fault,' she confessed, taking a glass of champagne from a passing waiter. 'I should have known better than to challenge him to tell the truth.'

Marsha bit her lip. 'I blame myself. I was so sure.'

Draining the glass, Kay drew a steadying breath and smiled brightly. 'Don't worry. I'm fine, really. This is supposed to be a party, so we'd better enjoy ourselves.'

Which she subsequently gave every sign of doing, amazing herself at her acting ability. Inside she was crying, but outside she was the life and soul of the party.

Only Marsha, with a deepening frown, knew that her youngest daughter was living a nightmare.

Yet worse was to come when the dancing started. There was no way that she could avoid dancing with Ben, though she managed to do so for as long as was possible. However, around midnight he cornered her, literally, taking the glass she held from her with grim determination.

'Don't fight me. I'm not enjoying this any more than you are. We'll have to dance at least once, or everyone will think it odd.' Taking her hand, he led her into the other room where the floor was alive with moving couples.

Kay shivered as he turned to her, but his hold was strictly formal, and to her relief they barely touched. She stared over his shoulder, a smile plastered to her face.

'Is Nita enjoying the party?' Somehow she couldn't resist probing her own open wound.

'Nita always enjoys parties,' he returned shortly.

'Bully for her!'

'Don't be bitchy, it doesn't become you.'

Kay sighed elaborately. 'I know, it's cheap. Like flinging myself at you. It's a habit I can't seem to get out of!'

'Try harder, damn it,' he gritted through his teeth. 'Now, as you value your life, shut up!'

They circled the floor in silence, Kay longing for the music to fade and bring an end to this torture. As they approached the windows for a second time, another couple collided with them, and all four came to a halt.

'Oops, sorry!' Connie apologised with a laugh, before a frown marred her brow. 'Good heavens, Ben, you never dance with any woman like that!' she declared on seeing the strictly formal hold he had on Kay.

'Mind your own business, Connie!' Ben advised through a tight smile.

'Suit yourself,' Connie returned huffily. 'But if I were you, I wouldn't make such a spectacle of yourself. I'm not the only one with eyes!' she added and swept her partner away.

'Damn her,' Ben exploded with a heartfelt groan, drawing Kay properly into his arms before she could resist.

She was forced to stifle a gasp, for it was an agony of delight to be this close. She could feel the awesome tension in him. He was hating every minute of it, and she squeezed her eyes tightly shut, her free hand balling into a fist on his shoulder.

Yet as the dance progressed, he suffered a sea-change. His movements became more fluid, more sensual. The hand at her waist spread out to imprint its warmth against her back. Finally his head lowered, lips brushing against her hair. Dazzled by the sensations this softening evoked, Kay melted helplessly against him. She knew it was madness, that it would only give her more pain, but she couldn't help herself. The world drifted away. There was only the two of them. Gradually the music grew fainter and fainter.

Only when Ben ceased moving did she open her eyes and blink up at him through the darkness. She realised then why the music came so faintly—he had steered them out on to the patio, down to where the shadows were at their deepest. Too vitally aware of him, Kay knew this was dangerous. However much she longed to stay, grab one final moment, it was wrong. Reluctantly she tried to break the spell he was weaving about them.

'Let me go, Ben,' she ordered, her voice sounding pained, and felt him shake his head.

'I can't—not yet.' His lips pressed hotly against her forehead. 'Why did you have to say it?' he groaned.

Her throat ached with suppressed tears. 'That I loved you? Because it was true.'

'I warned you how it was. How it must be. I never meant to hurt you.'

A tear escaped. Oh, Ben, we could have had it all, if only you'd loved me enough, she thought despairingly. 'You're hurting me now. If you don't want me, you've got to let me go. It's too cruel to do this to me, Ben. You've got to make up your mind once and for all.' It broke her heart to say it, but it was the only way.

His hands released her, framing her head, tipping it back so that the faint light revealed her pale face. 'Kay...' Her name was a groan, before his lips crushed hers in a kind of desperation. Then she was free. 'I'm sorry,' he said softly, and turned on his heel and strode away.

Kay pressed a trembling hand to her lips. She'd made him choose, and now he'd gone. The anguish of that last kiss was a revelation. Nothing else could have convinced her so strongly that he did love her, yet not enough to forget the past and take a risk. Marsha had been right, but there was to be no happy ending. He'd run all his life and was still running, and there was absolutely nothing she could do about it.

CHAPTER TEN

ONE month later, Kay let herself into her flat after a long day at work, and sank gratefully into the nearest armchair. She felt worn out. In fact, these days she always seemed to be tired. Probably because she had little or no appetite and was sleeping badly.

She tried not to think of the reason for that, because there was no point tormenting herself, and yet it seemed a hundred times a day that his face swam before her memory, and any progress she had made towards forgetting would be gone.

Sighing, she got up again, and went through to her kitchen, making herself a cup of coffee. Her mail lay unopened on the counter where she had left it that morning, and she rifled through it absently. There was a letter from Marsha, and that brought a smile to her lips as she opened it.

They had been corresponding since she had come home, by letter and telephone. In the short time they had been together, they had developed a close relationship, which gave Kay that much needed sense of belonging. Since her return, she had seen quite a bit of Connie and Sir Charles, too, generally dining with them at least once a week.

Marsha's letter was full of family chatter, and it lifted Kay's spirits, but at the end there was a note that brought a return of her frown. Because her mother knew about Kay's last meeting with Ben, she had been careful not to mention him, but now Marsha was asking if she had seen anything of him.

Kay felt a fluttering of nerves in her stomach. He couldn't be ill, could he? Almost immediately she stiffened her spine. Why should she be worrying? He had made it patently clear that he didn't want that kind of thing from her, she thought, with a touch of bitterness. And that, of course, brought irritatingly weak tears to the backs of her eyes. She couldn't change her nature, couldn't be hard however much she wanted to. Loving someone, even if they refused to accept it, meant caring what happened to them.

Oh, why had Marsha had to raise Ben's spectre again? It had been hard enough deciding it was best to try and forget him. It hadn't stopped her heart from aching. It had been aching ever since.

However, deciding to forget and doing so were not the same thing. Which was why she spent a virtually sleepless night worrying, and went to meet her grandfather for lunch at his club next day, determined to learn more. Not an easy prospect, for her refusal to discuss Ben had been the cause of the one and only argument between them.

They chatted easily, and it was only after they had been served with slices of raspberry pavlova that she finally broached the subject closest to her heart. Toying with her spoon, Kay cleared her throat and plunged in.

'How is Ben these days?'

Sir Charles was silent for so long that she eventually had to look up, only to find him regarding her speculatively.

'Is that just a polite query, my dear, or do you really want to know?'

Her eyes widened. He had a very succinct way of expressing his disapproval. 'Grandfather!' she exclaimed reproachfully.

Sir Charles sighed ruefully. 'I'm sorry, Kay, of course I know you care. I simply find it hard watching him drive himself the way he does.'

'Can't you stop him?' she asked, frowning.

His laugh was grim. 'Have you ever tried to stop a raging bull? He won't listen to me. In fact, I scarcely see him at all these days, unless business demands it. I was hoping that you might be able to do something.'

Kay recoiled instantly, her face looking pinched. 'Why me? Surely it's Nita you should ask.'

'Fiddlesticks! I doubt if he's clapped eyes on Nita from that day to this. He wouldn't have had the time! It's work, work, work with him, and if it goes on this way he'll kill himself,' Sir Charles declared pointedly.

Kay glanced away and jolted with shock as her disbelieving eyes beheld Ben walking towards them. All at once her heart began to thud wildly and she could feel herself trembling. One look was enough to tell her her grandfather was right. There was a tightness to his face, a grimness in his expression. The suit that had once been like a second skin now sat loosely on him. When he stopped beside them, she could only stare.

'Charles, I thought I'd find you here,' he greeted tersely, before turning to Kay. 'I stopped by to tell you the police have apprehended Ronnie Napier. He was trying to leave the country.'

She swallowed, unlocking her voice, which had frozen with his arrival. 'Oh! Th-that's good news,' she muttered helplessly.

His hands flexed, then disappeared into his trouser pockets. 'Apparently, in his statement, Ronnie says he telephoned his wife several weeks ago, but that you answered, and told him she had died. Is that true?'

Kay's lips formed an 'O' of surprise. 'That was him? I didn't realise. I'd almost forgotten about it, that's why I never thought to mention it to you. There were some clippings which he must have sent, too, but I don't understand why.'

'For money, of course. He had run out. Jean was his only available source, and he intended threatening to implicate her if she refused to help him get more. Her death put an end to that.'

'Poor Mum, I'm glad she never knew. But in an odd way, I suppose I have to thank Ronnie. If he hadn't tried blackmail, I never would have found my real family,' Kay said softly.

'They say every cloud has a silver lining,' Ben observed shortly, straightening up.

Seeing him about to move away, Kay caught hold of his arm, eyes searching his. 'How are you, Ben?' she asked huskily.

Easing away so that she was forced to release him, he smiled. 'Fine. Working hard as usual.'

It was clear from his tone that he wanted the conversation kept brief, but there was something she had to ask. 'And Nita? She's well?'

'Nita's always blooming, but I'll tell her you've been asking after her.' Shooting back his cuff, he glanced at his watch. 'I have to go. I'll see you later, Charles.' For one brief moment, his eyes locked with hers. 'Take care of yourself, Kay,' he advised, then with a brief nod was gone.

Kay's shoulders slumped. 'So, he's still seeing Nita,' she said flatly.

'The boy's a damn fool! You're worth a hundred of her,' Sir Charles harrumphed. 'Eat your dessert before it gets cold,' he ordered, doing likewise.

Laughing through a mist of tears, Kay reached across to take his hand. 'Oh, Grandfather, you're priceless,' she proclaimed, then bit her lip. 'What am I going to do?'

Sir Charles looked disheartened. 'I only wish I knew, my dear. I only wish I knew,' he admitted gruffly, and squeezed her hand encouragingly.

Kay sighed and stared at the door, left with the haunting vision of him walking away from her again.

* * *

Kay found it hard to concentrate for the rest of the day, and eventually went home knowing she had to start the forgetting process all over again.

It was a warm evening, and she went round throwing the windows wide to let fresh air into what felt like her own Turkish bath. Then she prepared herself a salad and sat eating it by the window while she listened to the news. Unfortunately that was as depressing as ever, and the lettuce was limp. She switched off the radio and scraped the remains of her meal into the bin.

About to go and run herself a bath, she was halted in her tracks by the ring of the doorbell. Suspecting it was one of her neighbours on the cadge, she went to answer it, only to find it was Lance outside her door.

'Hello, Kay,' he greeted her stiffly. 'I was just passing and saw your light. I've been meaning to speak to you. Can I come in for a moment?'

As their parting had not been pleasant, Kay stepped back reluctantly. It was only good manners that suggested she should hear him out. 'Come in.'

In the lounge, she watched him sit down and wondered how she could ever have contemplated marrying him. She felt nothing, save a mild aversion. Lance cleared his throat nervously.

'I wanted to apologise. I wasn't very fair to you that day. Knowing who you are, now, I realise I should have been more understanding. Don't misunderstand me, I'm not trying to get back into your life. In fact, there's someone else now. We're thinking of getting engaged.' He passed on this bit of information with an embarrassed smile. 'The thing is, I always liked you, Kay, and my conscience wouldn't let me rest until I'd apologised.'

It reminded her that there had been things about him she liked, and so she smiled. 'It's really not necessary, but thank you. I'm glad to hear you've found someone else. Would you like a cup of coffee? You can tell me all about her.'

He took up the offer eagerly, and Kay realised that that was probably the stronger reason for his coming here. While she was in the kitchen, the telephone rang.

'I'll get it,' Lance called out, and she heard him talking.

As she carried the cups through, she frowned at seeing the receiver back on its rest. 'Who was it?'

'Wrong number. Wanted to know who I was, and hung up when I gave my name,' Lance explained.

As it happened regularly, Kay soon forgot about it. They talked for over an hour, but it was clear that they had very little in common these days. When he left, Kay wished him well and knew they wouldn't meet again. Belatedly she went to take her bath and wash her hair, emerging to don a white lacy teddy and slip her silk thigh-length kimono over the top. In this humidity, it was the most comfortable thing she had to wear.

She wandered around, tidying up, then was just considering curling up with a book when the doorbell rang again. Not only rang, but continued to ring as whoever was out there kept his or her finger on the button.

'All right, all right, I'm coming,' she called irritably as the noise went on, tightening the belt of her kimono. It ceased as she rattled the chain. 'Who is it?' she called through the door.

There was a sound of muttering, then, 'Who the hell do you think?' in tones that didn't bode well.

'Ben?' Shocked surprise made her freeze, then with a fast-beating heart she fumbled with the latch. Throwing the door wide, she faced her unexpected visitor.

Her first thought was he had been home. The suit was gone, and in its place he wore jeans and an open-necked shirt. It flattered his lean look, giving him an earthy sensuality, and as that physical appeal bombarded her senses she caught sight of his face and gasped silently. He looked positively haggard. There were lines about his mouth, and shadows under his eyes.

'My God, you look awful!' she exclaimed weakly.

His lip curled. 'Whereas you...' Abruptly he stopped as he took stock of exactly how she looked. Utterly feminine, intensely sensual, and far, far too inviting. 'Hell, he's still here, isn't he?' Ben charged thickly, and, without giving her time to protest, brushed her aside and marched in.

Temper rising, Kay slammed the door, careless of the neighbours, and followed him. 'You've got a nerve, barging in here as if you owned the place!' she challenged.

Ben took not one ounce of notice. 'Where is he? In the bedroom?'

Crossing her arms, Kay watched him disappear into that room like a mini tornado, only to reappear again far more circumspectly. Staring at her furious figure, he dragged a hand through his hair.

'He isn't here.'

Temper rising still further, she ground her teeth. 'Who isn't here?'

Blue eyes speared her to the spot. 'How many lovers do you have, so you can't keep track of them?'

She gasped, colouring. 'How dare you come here throwing those sort of accusations about? There was nobody here, plural or singular!'

Ben's hands braced against his hips, his whole posture accusing. 'Lance was. Or are you going to tell me I imagined him answering the phone?'

Kay blinked, lips parting. 'It was you on the phone? Why did you hang up?'

His jaw flexed, and he breathed in deeply. 'It's not important, and it doesn't matter where lover-boy is; you aren't going to marry him, is that clear?'

Her heart fluttered with a mixture of emotions, hope warring with annoyance at his arbitrary command. 'Oh, yes? Says who?' she threw back, experiencing a thrill of excitement at the look in his eyes as he came towards her.

'I say. The man's nothing but a fortune-hunter, and you're a babe in the woods. You need protecting from him and others like him!'

Kay, going from anger to anticipation in the space of a few seconds, had never felt less like arguing, but she couldn't stop now, not until she knew exactly what he meant. 'Is that so? And who's going to do the job? You?' she scoffed.

His eyes narrowed. 'Can you think of anyone better?'

She couldn't, actually. 'My grandfather.'

'He's too old.'

'Peter, then.'

'He's too young, besides being on the wrong side of the Atlantic,' Ben countered swiftly.

In silence, Kay faced him out. 'You're saying you're the *only* man for the job?' she asked, hands going to her hips, unaware that the belt had slipped, allowing the kimono to part, revealing the fetching sight beneath.

Ben didn't miss it. The colour of his eyes deepened, and his lips gently curved as he relaxed slightly. 'The only man for you,' he corrected huskily, and her nerves went haywire. 'If you didn't dress that way for Lance, who did you dress for?' he went on huskily, eyes running over her lazily.

With a gasp Kay glanced down, hot colour storming into her cheeks as she realised how she looked. Automatically her hands went to her belt, but Ben caught her wrists, holding them apart, stopping her. Breathing restricted, Kay met his eyes.

'I didn't dress for anyone. I've just had a bath and washed my hair.'

At the admission, Ben took a step closer. 'You have very sexy underwear, but I don't like the idea of anyone else seeing it.'

Her insides began turning molten as the air around them started to seethe and boil. 'My husband may have something to say about that,' she argued huskily.

Ben shook his head. 'No, I don't think he will. Because the only man you're going to marry is me,' he declared softly. 'You see, protecting you from fortune-hunters is going to be a full-time job, and the only way I can do it is to marry you.'

With her heart thudding wildly, Kay found it difficult to concentrate, especially when his eyes continued to caress her so blatantly. 'Aren't you forgetting something? You're going to marry Nita.'

'You know I could never have married her, not if I lived to be a hundred,' he declared simply.

She couldn't quite hide the pain in her eyes at that. 'Do I?'

Gently, Ben raised her right hand to his lips and pressed a kiss to her palm, sending *frissons* of pleasure along her veins. 'You've always known it, long before I did. Say you'll marry me,' he urged thickly.

She swallowed hard. 'So that you can protect me?'

He shook his head. 'To save me from going out of my mind.'

Suddenly her lips were dry, and she had to moisten them. 'There's only one reason I'll marry you, Ben. Because I love you. So now is the time to run, if you've a mind to.'

To her joy, he shook his head. 'I'm not going to run any more. I always thought I couldn't live with that emotion, but now I find that what I can't live without is you. I'll take whatever you give me. I *need* you.'

Emotion swamped her. Those three words said *so* much. He was giving at last, and there was no way she could refuse because one word was missing. 'Then my answer is yes, Ben.'

He looked for a moment as if he couldn't believe it, then with a groan he swept her into his arms, burying his face against the tender skin of her shoulder as her arms encircled his neck and clung tightly. Then his hands lifted to frame her head and draw it back so that he could look into her eyes.

'Dear God, I never meant to hurt you,' he apologised thickly.

She smiled through tears of joy. 'I know,' she whispered.

'Do you know why I rang? Because I wanted to hear your voice. *Needed* to hear it,' he admitted with a groan. 'I stayed away as long as I could, and then today it suddenly hit me. What the hell was I doing? Nothing I did meant anything without you. I had to see you again. That's why I went to the club. Telling you about Ronnie was just an excuse.'

'Oh, Ben, I'm so glad you came, whatever the excuse.'

'I haven't seen Nita, either, not since the party. I couldn't. All she did was remind me she wasn't you. There could never, ever be any other woman but you for me.'

Gently he traced her face with tender kisses, her eyes, her cheeks, her chin—until finally his lips met hers, yet trembling as if he was afraid that he might hurt her. Kay's heart turned over. Marsha had said he was capable of a great love, and she felt it in him now, in his restraint and caring. She could feel his wanting of her in every straining sinew, but what he felt was so much more than that, transcending the physical. She knew if she looked at him she would see the glow that her own eyes reflected.

Yet as the seconds passed, that no longer became enough, for either of them. The passion that had always been there between them sprung into vibrant life. As her fingers glided into his thick hair, his kisses deepened, his tongue seeking hers, igniting the embers that sent fire licking along their veins. Her sigh of pleasure caught in her throat as his hands brushed the kimono from her shoulders, dropping it to the floor, and found the soft skin beneath.

Kay buried her face in his neck, shivering at the delicious spirals his increasingly bold caresses evoked deep inside her. She could feel him trembling and that excited her unbearably, to know that she could bring that strong, proud man to this. Her fingers fumbled with his shirt and he pulled back, shrugging out of it. She would have reached for him then, but he stopped her. Trembling fingers brushed the lace straps of her teddy aside, peeling it from her slowly, his eyes making her flesh burn.

Then the silk scrap fell away and his hands cupped her breasts, their burgeoning nipples thrusting into his palms. Pleasure shot through her, and her head fell back. Her eyes closed. She hadn't known she could feel so wanton, so aroused. It was glorious and she wanted Ben to feel it too. Her head came up and her hands sought the silken hair on his chest, searching out the flat male nipples, delighting as she felt him shudder.

When he took her in his arms again, the feel of her breasts against his strong chest made her groan out her need, and then he was sweeping her up, carrying her into the bedroom to lay her gently on the bed, waiting only to remove the last of his clothes before joining her. Then the world spun away. There was only sensation as limbs locked and two silken bodies gloried in the freedom to worship each other. The only sounds were broken moans and sighs of delight, and words of love. Coming together as one, they were transported into a spiralling whirlpool of almost unbearable pleasure. Until finally they toppled over the edge, clinging together as the world exploded around them.

Coming reluctantly back to earth, Kay felt replete, so full that she wanted to cry. When Ben raised himself above her, his eyes gleamed like jewels, and she knew he had been as moved as she.

'How could I ever have believed I could live without you?' he asked gruffly.

From somewhere came the strength to laugh. 'I don't know. How could you?'

With a groan of self-disgust, Ben turned on to his side, and she moved to face him. He pulled a face, one finger tracing the kiss-swollen line of her lips.

'Of course, you know I love you, don't you?' It wasn't so much a question as a statement of fact. Yet it brought the tears to her eyes.

'Of course. Everybody did. You were the last to know,' she joked, feeling that life could not possibly offer her more than this moment had.

'Marsha! She always knew me better than anyone. I suppose she told you about my family?' Ben asked, smoothing her tangled hair from her face.

'Mmm. That's why I understood, even if I didn't like it,' Kay admitted.

'No woman had ever fought so hard for me,' he declared in wonder. 'You turned my world upside-down, but I was scared,' Ben sighed. 'I never wanted to feel that kind of pain again. That's why I ran when I realised you'd got too close. But instead I put myself through hell. I meant to treat you like another sister, but I couldn't think of you that way. Save myself!' he exclaimed with a harsh laugh. 'All I did was make it worse, because this time I brought it on myself.

'I tried to use Nita, but that was madness. Then I tried to use work to forget you. What a fool! Are you sure you want to marry me?'

'Absolutely.'

'That means we're probably both mad!' he said, not displeased at the thought. 'Anyway, I was prepared to eat humble pie in order to win you back. Then I telephoned and Lance answered, and...' Abruptly Ben broke off, backing away a little and avoided her eyes.

Her eyes widened surprise. 'Ben? You're blushing!'

Gritting his teeth, he edged further away. 'Don't be ridiculous!'

'You are! What happened? Tell me. You can't leave it there!' Still he didn't answer. She advanced on him with the glow of vengeance in her eyes, determined to get at the truth. Ben backed away rapidly. So much so that he fell off the edge of the bed and cracked his head on the floor. When he looked up, Kay was leaning over the edge, biting her lip in a mainly unsuccessful attempt to stop laughing.

'Serves you right!'

Rubbing his head, he glared at her balefully. 'Help me up.' He held out a hand which she ignored.

'Oh, no, I rather like seeing you down there.'

'It's cold,' he protested.

'The humidity in here takes my breath away.'

'Hell, if you're going to be like that, I don't think I'll marry you after all!' he grumbled.

She grinned down at him. 'After you've gone to so much trouble to get me? After the incredible love-making we just shared? And which we won't share again unless you tell me the truth,' she threatened.

'You're a hard task-master, Kay Endacott! All right. The truth is, when I heard Lance's voice, I thought I could get you back without having to eat crow.'

Kay frowned wrathfully. 'Chauvinist!'

His blue eyes danced. 'Hate me?'

Laughing exasperatedly, she slipped over the side and joined him. 'You only told me because you know I'd forgive you anything.' His arms had welcomed her and now his fingers were foraging in mind-blowing fashion, making it impossible to stay aloof. 'You're incorrigible!'

His lips nuzzled her neck. 'If that means I'm in love, I admit it. What more do you want?'

With a smile that was pure seduction, Kay bent and whispered in his ear.

He chuckled sexily. 'Now who's incorrigible?' he exclaimed, and claimed her lips in a kiss that left room for nothing but love.

ANNOUNCING THE

FLYAWAY VACATION SWEEPSTAKES!

This month's destination:

Beautiful SAN FRANCISCO!

This month, as a special surprise, we're offering an exciting FREE VACATION!

Think how much fun it would be to visit San Francisco "on us"! You could ride cable cars, visit Chinatown, see the Golden Gate Bridge and dine in some of the finest restaurants in America!

The facing page contains two Entry Coupons (as does every book you received this shipment). Complete and return *all* the entry coupons; **the more times you enter, the better your chances of winning!**

Then keep your fingers crossed, because you'll find out by June 15, 1995 if you're the winner! If you are, here's what you'll get:

- Round-trip airfare for two to beautiful San Francisco!
- 4 days/3 nights at a first-class hotel!
- $500.00 pocket money for meals and sightseeing!

Remember: The more times you enter, the better your chances of winning!*

FLYAWAY VACATION
SWEEPSTAKES
OFFICIAL ENTRY COUPON

This entry must be received by: MAY 30, 1995
This month's winner will be notified by: JUNE 15, 1995
Trip must be taken between: JULY 30, 1995-JULY 30, 1996

YES, I want to win the San Francisco vacation for two. I understand the prize includes round-trip airfare, first-class hotel and $500.00 spending money. Please let me know if I'm the winner!

Name_____

Address _____ Apt. _____

City   State/Prov.   Zip/Postal Code

Account #_____

Return entry with invoice in reply envelope.

© 1995 HARLEQUIN ENTERPRISES LTD.   CSF KAL

FLYAWAY VACATION
SWEEPSTAKES
OFFICIAL ENTRY COUPON

This entry must be received by: MAY 30, 1995
This month's winner will be notified by: JUNE 15, 1995
Trip must be taken between: JULY 30, 1995-JULY 30, 1996

YES, I want to win the San Francisco vacation for two. I understand the prize includes round-trip airfare, first-class hotel and $500.00 spending money. Please let me know if I'm the winner!

Name_____

Address _____ Apt. _____

City   State/Prov.   Zip/Postal Code

Account #_____

Return entry with invoice in reply envelope.

© 1995 HARLEQUIN ENTERPRISES LTD.   CSF KAL